Charles Wells

Mehemet the Kurd

And other Tales from Eastern Sources

Charles Wells

Mehemet the Kurd
And other Tales from Eastern Sources

ISBN/EAN: 9783337137656

Printed in Europe, USA, Canada, Australia, Japan

Cover: Foto ©Andreas Hilbeck / pixelio.de

More available books at **www.hansebooks.com**

MEHÉMET, THE KURD,

AND

OTHER TALES,

FROM

EASTERN SOURCES.

BY

CHARLES WELLS,

TURKISH PRIZEMAN OF KING'S COLLEGE, LONDON, AND MEMBER OF THE ROYAL
ASIATIC SOCIETY.

———————

LONDON:

BELL AND DALDY,

186, FLEET STREET, AND 6, YORK STREET, COVENT GARDEN.
1865.

LONDON:
CLAYTON AND CO., PRINTERS,
BOUVERIE STREET.

TO

WILLIAM COOK, ESQ.,

OF

SOUTH NORWOOD,

AS

A TOKEN OF FRIENDSHIP,

THIS WORK

IS

𝔇𝔢𝔡𝔦𝔠𝔞𝔱𝔢𝔡,

BY

THE AUTHOR.

PREFACE.

————◆————

THE following tales, which are now published, were translated by me whilst I was engaged in the study of Eastern languages. They have lain in my desk for several years, and I should never have ventured to bring them to the light, had I not been strongly urged to do so by those who had read the manuscript.

Wishing to give the English reader some idea of the novel style of these Eastern tales, I have, especially in the principal story, purposely retained many peculiarities which may make the language sound somewhat un-English. I must, therefore, claim the indulgence of the public for any faults of style they may notice, considering the difficulty I had to contend with in translating from languages so different from our own, especially as I wished not to completely denationalize the tales, but to preserve, to a certain extent, the strange mixture of rugged simplicity and gorgeous extravagance of the original.

With regard to the verses appended, I must forewarn the reader that I give them only as imitations of Eastern poetry, the metre of which is very irregular and peculiar. Judged as English poems, I am perfectly aware they may be found defective; but as attempts at free metrical translations of Eastern verse, they might, I flattered myself, be of interest, and be looked on indulgently.

The immense success which attended the publication of the "Thousand and One Nights," which book is a translation of a collection of popular Eastern tales, led me to think that the English public might peruse with interest other Eastern tales. Those which I have selected, I believe, have never before been made known in England; and the principal tale, which is an Arabic manuscript, has never been translated into any European language.

CONTENTS.

	PAGE
The Story of Mehemet, the Kurd	1
The Princess and the Cobbler	95
The Disputed Maiden	104
The Invincibleness of Love	110
The Prince Tailor	116
The Wife with Two Husbands	121
The Tale of a Skull	128
Turkish Proverbs	132
A Turkish Love-Letter	135

ORIENTAL POETRY—	137
The Rose and the Nightingale	143
Nuvaz and Bazenda	164
Love's Power	171
The Lover to his Heart	172
The Lover's Farewell	173
Turkish Love-Song	174
The Butterfly and the Candle	175
Serve that King whose Empire knoweth no Decay	176
The Merry Spring	177
The Mussulman and the Christian Maid	180
The Lover's Address to the Love-Letter	182

THE STORY

OF

MEHEMET, THE KURD.

———◁∞▷———

THE Arabic historians relate that many years ago there
lived a man of the tribe of the Kurds, of an ancient and
illustrious family called Ker Khan. He was of the nomads,
and encamped in the desert, where he was one of the greatest
chiefs. God had granted him abundant riches—great num-
bers of horses, camels, sheep, and cattle of all kinds—and he
showed himself grateful towards God, and appreciated his
favours; for his greatest pleasure was in doing good, and he
gave much alms to the poor.

Now be it known, the tribe of Ker Khan passed the
greater part of the year in the neighbourhood of Aleppo, a
charming country where water and pasture are in abundance.

One year, by the will of God, the country was desolated
by a dreadful famine, and the inhabitants were obliged to
travel to other lands for subsistence. Ker Khan was amongst
those who left the country, accompanied by the whole of his
tribe. They travelled from country to country, and from land
to land, until they came to Persia; and, loving to wander

thus, and to change their abode each day to some new spot, they arrived at last on the borders of India.

Here they found water and pasture in abundance, and it being a charming country they settled in that part, and continued on the confines of India for many years.

One day, whilst they were in this neighbourhood, as Ker Khan was tranquilly smoking his pipe at the door of his tent, he began to think of his native land, and how that now, when his hair was beginning to grow grey, he had no child, male or female, to inherit his riches; and the thought of this gave him great sorrow, and grief oppressed him. At night, when he retired to rest, still occupied by this sad reflection, he turned from side to side unable to sleep, and at last arose and left the tent, and repaired to a spring not far from there, from which the tribe drew water. The night was beautiful, the sky serene, and the moon and stars were shining in the heavens. Ker Khan having come to the spring, performed his ablutions, and then began to pray as follows :—"O Lord my God, Creator of heaven and earth, Thou who seest all, but art invisible, I pray and conjure Thee by Thy Omnipotence to have pity on me, and grant me a child to inherit my riches after my death. I ask this favour from Thy infinite goodness." Having finished praying he returned to his tent, and God having heard his prayer, his wife conceived; and after four months her state became known, and every one rejoiced. Then Ker Khan rejoiced also, and gave alms to the poor, and did great acts of charity.

One night, shortly after this, as he was sleeping, Ker Khan saw a vision, in which an angel came to him and said, "O Ker Khan, know that thy wife is with child, and that she will bear a son who will be renowned, who will govern men, and will be the chief of a great nation. When he is born give him the name of Mehemet."

When Ker Khan awoke he was greatly rejoiced, and thanked God, and kept the affair secret. In due time his wife bore a child, beautiful as the moon; and he gave a banquet and invited every one, and gave charity to the poor, and his house was open to all for a whole month. He spared neither trouble nor money in the education of the child, and when he was seven years old he sent for a professor to teach him caligraphy and to read the Koran; and Mehemet made great progress in both.

Unfortunately, however, he had too much the character of the Kurds and the inhabitants of the desert, who are extraordinarily simple.

When he was twelve years old he lost his father, Ker Khan, and was greatly afflicted, and interred him with great pomp. He inherited all his father's wealth—all the horses, camels, and cattle—and began to make friends with the young people of his own age, whom he invited to his house, and who came and partook of his bounty, and enjoyed themselves at his expense. His mother, whom he loved tenderly, did not prevent him from incurring such great expenses. Four years had not passed before he lost all his wealth. When he came to the age of manhood he lost his mother, and remained alone. His mother had done all she could to get him married, but he had always refused, being entirely taken up by his friends. After the death of his mother he increased his wastefulness, until after a short time scarcely anything remained. Then he began to sell the sheep, the camels, and the horses, to feast his friends with. At the age of twenty-one he had nothing but his tent. The friends of his father attempted to arrest him in this course, but he accepted not their counsels; he even sold the furniture of his tent; and when one day he had nothing to eat, as he who has acquired a habit cannot break it, he sold the large tent he had, and only kept a small tent for a single person. Afterwards he sold the clothes which his mother and father had given him; and now his friends, who saw that he had nothing remaining, began to withdraw, and soon those whom he had feasted did not even deign to salute him when he passed their tents—avoided meeting him, or pretended not to see him. He became so poor that he went three days without eating or drinking. He experienced all the horrors of poverty, and at last, half dead with hunger, thought he would go and see some of his friends, not doubting that they would give him something to eat. He went and stood at a certain distance from their tent—his feelings not allowing him to approach nearer—when one of his most intimate friends passed by him without paying him the least attention, and without asking him to eat anything with him. When he saw this his tears began to fall, and he felt the greatest indignation at such conduct; he returned mortified to his little tent, which was at a great distance from the others, for his friends, whose friendship had changed into hatred against him, whenever he wished to pitch his tent amongst them, drove him away, saying, "Do not let that unlucky fellow come near us;" and therefore it was that his tent was at a great distance from the others.

Disappointed and dejected, he went and sat down in his tent, and began to weep bitterly. Now, one of the old friends of his father happened to pass by that spot, and heard him weeping and moaning, and entered; and when he saw the miserable state he was in, he remembered the many kindnesses his father had done him, and began to weep also, and began to console him, saying, "My dear son, do not give yourself up to grief thus, for men are always the plaything of fortune, which now elevates them, now casts them down; and man must show courage in adversity, and behave with fortitude in all circumstances. I would give you money, but I fear that would not last long with you. Come, however, to me, and you shall not want for food." The young man refused, and continued to weep until the kind heart of the good man was touched, and he wept with him, and took him by force home with him, and, after having given him something to eat and drink, said to him, "My dear son, do not give yourself up to grief, for God forgets no one. I offer you a bed · and a place at my table until God changes your condition for a better." The young man answered, "As you insist on keeping me with you, I am very grateful, and I beg of you to take me as your servant or as the least of your shepherds." —"No, no," replied the old man; "you shall be like one of my children, and God will forget neither you nor me."— "Then," said the young man, "I will remain with you, but on condition of tending your flocks." To satisfy him, the good old man consented.

Early the next morning the young man arose, took the sheep, and went to lead them to pasture. Filled with poignant grief, his tears flowed down his cheeks, and he could not forget his misfortune. Whenever he thought of his former greatness and of his present miserable state, he could not help weeping, and was inconsolable.· This state of things continued for a long time, when one day the shepherds came together, and began bantering with one another until at last they quarrelled. Mehemet tried to interfere to separate them,

and to reconcile them. Then one of them struck him, and
began to swear at him; and Mehemet, who was not used to
being struck or swore at, was so mortified that all the world
seemed black to his eyes. However, he swallowed his grief;
but when at the end of the day he returned home, his master
saw that tears were falling down his cheeks. "What is the
matter, my dear son, and what makes you weep?" he asked.
"Nothing," replied Mehemet; "but I do not wish to remain
any longer here. I have nothing to detain me, and I want to
see the world, and escape from the insults heaped on me by
the inhabitants of this country."—"You are only twenty years
of age," said the old man; "how can you go into countries
where you have never been, and whose inhabitants are
strangers to you? I am not forgetful of the benefits which
your father did me, and I speak as an old friend of your
father; if you leave this country you will break my heart."—
"I am very sensible of the interest you take in me," replied
Mehemet, "but nothing can dissuade me from my intention
to travel. I would rather die and be buried than suffer so
many mortifications in this country."—"But tell me, then,
what has happened," said the old man. Now, Mehemet was
too proud to say that he had been struck by a shepherd, and
remained silent, delivered the flock over to the old man, bade
him farewell, and prepared to set out for the desert. Then
the good old man besought him to stop, and said to him,
"Since you are not to be shaken in your resolution of leaving,
at least accept these five sheep in return for your services;
when you come to a village you can sell them, and live on
the price until God send you something else."—"No, no,"
replied Mehemet; "I cannot accept them, for if I could
keep them I should have kept those which my father left

me." But the old man insisted until Mehemet was obliged
to accept the five sheep, which he drove before him. The
old man also made him accept provisions for his journey. So
he set out, and, after having walked all day, passed the night
on the bank of a river, reflecting bitterly on his condition.
The next day he went on, driving the five sheep before him,
and continued to do thus for five days; but in this way he
proceeded very slowly, and regretted having accepted the five
sheep, and looked around for some one to whom to give
them, for he did not wish to leave them in the desert, out of
pity for them. While he was thus thinking, he perceived a
man at a distance walking quickly, and cried out to him;
and the man having turned, saw that it was a young Kurd
man who called him. Then he said to himself, "By Allah!
the Kurds are a stupid people. What is to hinder me from
getting these five sheep?" So he went to Mehemet and
asked him what he wanted; and Mehemet asked the man
whence he came and whither he was going. The man
answered, "I come from my country and from the country I
belong to : as to the place I am going to, I will not tell it to
any one." Then Mehemet conjured him by the Prophet to
tell him whither he was going; and the man said, "Since
you conjure me by the Prophet, I must tell it you. Know,
then, that yesterday I had a dream, and now I am going to
catch it before any one can take it before me." When
Mehemet heard these words he was astonished; and being
very simple, as we have said, he thought that a dream must
be something to eat or drink. So he said to the man,
"Will you not sell me your dream?"—"Yes, with great
pleasure," answered the man; and as Mehemet wished to get
rid of the five sheep, and the man wished to get them, they

were not long in coming to an agreement. So Mehemet gave
the man the five sheep, and asked him what he was to do to
catch the dream. The man said, "Take this stick and this bag
of provisions, follow this road, and walk very quickly; towards
evening you will come to the gate of a city—there you will
catch the dream which is waiting for you. I congratulate you
on the bargain you have got; but I counsel you to go quickly,
or another may be before you and catch the dream."

Here we must state that the man pointed to a path leading he knew not whither, in order that Mehemet might lose
himself in the desert, and that he might have time to escape
with the five sheep before Mehemet could return.

Mehemet walked on all day. Towards evening he sat down
under a tree, and passed the night there. The next morning
he saw that he was in the midst of an immense desert, and
knew not which way to turn; and having eaten all the provisions he had with him, he began to eat the herbs and roots
which he found near, and to drink the rain-water collected in
the fissures of the rocks. Thus he passed five days, constantly
walking onwards. The sixth day he beheld a very high
mountain, and having climbed up to the top, he looked
around on all sides, and saw at a great distance behind the
mountain a great city, in the midst of an extensive plain, surrounded by gardens, running streams, and trees loaded with
fruit. Notwithstanding he was very weak and exhausted
with hunger and fatigue, he descended the side of the mountain, and took the road to the city, but did not arrive there
until near nightfall. He saw that it was a well-fortified
town, of stately appearance, with towers and palaces, surrounded by spacious gardens, in which streams of water
wound on all sides. When he arrived at the gate of the city

he found he was too late to enter, and that the gate was closed ; and as it was in winter-time, and he wished to find shelter, he went all round the town, but without meeting any one.   At last, as it was beginning to get very dark, he said to himself, " I will go into one of the gardens and pass the night, and to-morrow will enter the city."   He had forgotten the dream which he was to catch, for he was more dead than alive from fatigue.   So having found a gate of one of the gardens open, he entered, and sat down beneath a tree. Scarcely had he sat down, when it began to thunder and lighten, and to rain in torrents.   As the cold was excessive, and the rain was falling fast, Ker Khan began to look around him to find some place where he could take shelter; and seeing a small hut in the garden, he went towards it, entered, and having lain himself down and covered himself with his shepherd's mantle, fell asleep.

We will now relate to the reader the history of the town outside which our hero was lying, and of the wonderful things which had taken place there.   The city was called " The City of the Four Towers," from the fact of there being four towers in it—one at each corner of the town.   The towers were built of bricks made of seven metals, cemented with copper and glass, and had been built by one of the wise men of olden times—a philosopher called Kidar.   This philosopher had invented a balloon of red gold, incrusted with precious stones, on which he had written all the talismans. When he wished he got into his balloon and travelled in the air as the mariner with his vessel on the sea.   In this way he could traverse a great distance in a short space of time, and without any danger.   Now this philosopher had four children, to whom he had taught magic, philosophy, and all the other sciences, so that they were most distinguished scholars. As for himself, since he had invented the balloon of gold, he had done nothing but go from one land to another to see the wonders of the world. When he wished to return home he had only to direct the balloon towards Greece—for that was his native land—and he was there in the twinkling of an eye.

One day his children said to him, " Dear father, we pray thee to allow each of us to build a town where we may live, we, our posterity, and our disciples."—" My dear children," said their father, " I will not consent to your being separate from one another; therefore, I will mount my golden balloon and go and seek a good locality, and will build a town consisting of four quarters, in which you and your people can live." His children thanked him, and he mounted immediately into his balloon of gold, and visited all quarters of the earth, until he arrived at the spot on which the city stood of which we are speaking, where finding that the water was abundant and the air excellent, he chose it for the abode of his children. Then he returned to his family, made them get up into the balloon, and directing his course towards this spot, showed them the ground, and told them that no spot was more suitable for building a town. In short, they were delighted with the place, and kissed the hand of their father as a sign of their gratitude. Then the father alighted from the balloon, and marked out a spot four *fersenks* long and four *fersenks* broad—sixteen square *fersenks*—and told his eldest son, whose name was Ptolemy, to build a tower of seven metals, and to fill the space of four square *fersenks*, which fell to his share, with houses for his people; and he did the same with all his children, charging them each to inhabit his own quarter, to govern it equitably, and not make encroachments on the other.

So, each of the sons commenced to build his quarter, and they commenced the same day and finished the same day, and in order to finish it quickly they had recourse to the genii. When the town was finished, they surrounded it with a wall, surmounted by towers of marble; and then they went, they and their families, to inhabit it. They planted gardens, and conducted water into the interior of the city by pipes. They constructed basins, public fountains, and baths, and each one governed his quarter. As for the father, he built a high tower in the midst of the city, surmounted by a magnificent cupola of steel, and on all affairs of importance the four sons consulted him. This state of things continued all their lives. After many ages, their posterity becoming extinct, the four jurisdictions were united under a single king, whose name was Hassan. This king had a daughter of incomparable loveliness, so beautiful as to shame the moon herself. The king, her father, who loved her tenderly, sent for a master to teach her the Koran, and afterwards she learnt philosophy, astrology, and magic; and as she had been told that there was a distinguished scholar in Upper China (which was not far from the city), she prayed her father to send for him, to complete her education. The king accordingly wrote him a letter, and he repaired at once to the city on the invitation of the king. This sage man, who was called Zirajjan, was master of every science, and was no less wise than learned; in a word, he was the most accomplished man in the world. King Hassan said to him, "I invited you to come here to teach my daughter astrology, and to perfect her in the other sciences."—"With great pleasure," replied the

scholar; "but, Sire, I regret that I shall not be able to remain
with you, as I have two pupils, daughters of kings, whose
education has been confided to me; if, however, you will
entrust your daughter to me, I will take the greatest care of
her." Then the king confided his daughter to the wise
man, and promised him great riches; but the scholar said,
"Sire, I want not riches, for in my capacity as one of the
most learned men of the time, it is in my power to have as
much wealth as I wish." So the king gave his daughter all
that she required, and entrusted her to the wise man, who
took her home with him.

We have said that the philosopher had two young princesses to educate; one was called Badr-el-Maha (the Moon of
Beauty), the other Nuzhat-ez-Zeman (or the Delight of the
Age). As for the daughter of King Hassan, she was called
Durat-el-Muluk (or the Pearl of Kings). The two first
princesses were daughters of two kings of China, and their
fathers had sent them to the wise man to learn astrology and
magic. Now the wise man loved Nuzhat-ez-Zeman more
than the others, and taught her much more; but the three
princesses had the greatest love for one another, and lived in
the greatest unity.

At the end of three years King Hassan sent for his
daughter Durat-el-Muluk, who had made great progress in
astrology and magic. As for Badr-el-Maha, she distinguished
herself in the science of discovering treasures; while Nuzhat-
ez-Zeman excelled the others in magic and in all the other
sciences, for, as we have said, she was the favourite of the
wise man.

Durat-el-Muluk, the daughter of King Hassan, who loved
her two companions tenderly, left them with regret; and at her

departure they all three shed tears, and said, "May fate grant
that we may one day meet, and live together under the same
roof in unity."

Durat-el-Muluk was welcomed by her father with the
greatest joy and the greatest kindness. She failed not to
eulogize the wise man, and said that he had acted towards
her as a father. King Hassan was greatly pleased, and sent
precious presents to the wise man for the good education he
had given his daughter.

Soon the fame of the beauty and rare qualities of this
princess spread abroad, and all the neighbouring kings sent
ambassadors to demand her in marriage for their sons; but
the king, her father, refused her to every one. Now the
princess had a cousin named Aksun, who loved her passionately. He asked her hand of her father, but the king had
ordered him to be told that he had no daughter to marry.
Then the cousin went and besought the great men of the
kingdom to intercede in his favour with the king, and the
great men prayed the king to give his daughter to Aksun;
but the king was immoveable, and said that the marriage
should never take place. The two cousins, however, loved
one another, and corresponded secretly. Aksun wrote a letter
to the princess, in which he complained of the obstinacy of
her father. She answered that he must not despair, and
that she would accept no other but him, and that he must
be patient until her father should yield. The unfortunate
lover, however, could not be resigned, and his heart was consumed by the fire of love. He repeated his solicitation with
the great men, and they interceded a second time for him;
but the king was so incensed that he swore that Aksun
should never marry his daughter. Then the cousin was in

despair, and wrote a letter to the daughter of the king, relating what had befallen him, and the princess wrote a reply to him, which ran thus:—

"My beloved Cousin,—After the repeated refusals which my father has given, it is evident he will never consent to our marriage. However, you must not despair. I have formed a plan, which I am about to put into execution, and which I will now communicate to you. I will fill two portmanteaus with precious stones, and put them on two horses, and quit the city by night in the disguise of a man. You must wait for me outside the city; we will go to a kingdom independent of our father, and there we will be married according to the law. We shall have enough to live on, and to pass a very agreeable life. Await me, therefore, in the garden which is by the side of the eastern tower. We will meet on the evening of the fifth day of the week; but you must leave in the day, as the gates of the city are closed to all but me after sunset." When Aksun received this letter he was rejoiced, and waited impatiently for the time to pass.

As for the princess Durat-el-Muluk, she got ready a letter as coming from her father, for the gate-keeper, which ran thus :—" The bearer of this, one of my viziers, leaves the city by my orders on an affair of importance; you are hereby charged to open the gate to him without delay." This letter was indispensable, as the gate-keeper had orders not to open the gate to any one after sunset but by the express orders of the king. Having written this letter, when the king retired to rest she entered his chamber, took his seal, and stamped the letter with it. Then she filled the two trunks with gold and jewels, put them on the two horses, dressed herself as a man, mounted on one of the horses, and led the other; and having arrived at the gate of the city when it was already dark, she presented the letter to the gate-keeper, who having read it, kissed it, and put it to his forehead, as is the custom in the East, and opened the gate immediately. The princess directed her course towards the garden, which was the place of rendezvous. By the mysterious decrees of fate, this was the same night Mehemet had arrived in the garden, and had lain down in the hut as we have related. Durat-el-Muluk thought that her cousin was in the garden and that he had been waiting for her all day.

As for Aksun (which name signifies "The Bringer of Misfortune," and which his uncle had given him, as he hated him, and on account of his bringing misfortune wherever he went), seeing the storm and the thunder and lightning, he thought that his cousin would not leave the town that night; and went to bed very early, saying to himself, "I prefer to lie in bed such a night as this to standing shivering with cold in a garden." The princess Durat-el-Muluk, on the contrary, when she saw the rain, only thought that it would be a better opportunity for executing her project; for, as it was wet and cold, every one had retreated home. Having sought her cousin in every part of the garden, she at last went to the hut, and finding a man lying on the ground snoring, she advanced towards him and whispered to him—"Arise, arise, Aksun! it is not now the time to sleep." When Mehemet heard her voice, he thought she said, "I am the dream," which words, in Arabic, resemble the others greatly. So he arose and went out from the hut with the princess. As it was dark, she could not distinguish his features, but noticed that he did not wear the costume of the country, and thought he had disguised himself. Then she gave him a brace of pistols and a scimitar, and bade him follow her and mount. So Mehemet took the pistols and put them in his girdle, girded on the scimitar, and mounted on horse-back without saying a word; and they left the garden and took the high road. As the storm became more and more violent, they galloped all the night without saying a word. The next morning the sun arose, the rain ceased, and the clouds dispersed, and they found themselves in an extensive plain, near a spring of water. Then the princess wished to alight to refresh herself and take breakfast, and turned to her companion, who she thought was her cousin; and when she saw that he was a young man who had neither moustache nor beard, she was struck dumb with astonishment. At last she said, "Who are you, and what are you?"—"I am Mehemet, to be sure," he replied. "What were you doing in the garden?" she asked. "I was sleeping, of course, for I knew not whither to go," said he. Then she saw that it was a mistake, and was greatly perplexed, for she knew not what to do. Seeing her dressed as a man, and as she had her face covered, Mehemet took her for a man, and said, "Good father, I am a Kurd: my story is very curious;" and he set about relating to her all the hardships he had suffered—how he had bought the dream for the five sheep, how he came to the city whose gates were shut, how he had entered the garden, and lastly, how he had gone into the hut and was in a deep sleep when she had aroused him and told him to get up. "Now," said he, "I arose and followed you; give me the dream, and let me go." When the princess Durat-el-Muluk heard this recital, she could not help smiling, and remained silent for a whole hour. At last she began to reflect, and said to herself, "It is the will of God; my object was to marry my cousin, but it appears that God does not wish it, and that fate ordains that I should wed another. If I return to my father's city, the affair will be discovered by my father and mother, and I then shall cut a sorry figure; there is no remedy but to resign myself to the will of God." Having pondered thus for some time, she turned towards Mehemet, and looked in his face, and found that he was of great beauty, but thin from fatigue, and poorly clad. Then she told him to dismount and come to the spring. So they both alighted and breakfasted, and fed their horses. When they had finished, she told him to take off his old garments, and he being very simple, as we have said, thought that she meant to rob him, and cried out, "Oh, my good father! what are you going to do with my old clothes? they are worn out, and not worth a groosh, and if you take them I shall die with cold."—"I do not wish to strip you," she replied; "I only wish to change your old clothes for new ones;" whereupon she opened her portmanteau, and drew forth a magnificent suit. Then he threw off his old clothes, and attired himself in the new, and he appeared a very handsome youth. His beauty attracted her attention, and the flame of love was kindled in her heart towards him. Then she took a bottle from the portmanteau, gave him to drink, and drank herself. As he drank the colour returned to his cheeks, and his eyes regained their brilliancy, till he seemed, to her eyes, to be more like a heavenly being than a mortal. She could do nothing but admire him, and soon forgot her cousin. Love made him appear to her to be the handsomest man in the world; and she said to herself, "What a handsome man! is he not a thousand times handsomer than my cousin? How I ought to thank Heaven for having granted me more than I expected." In short, she was delighted, but concealed her joy.

Mehemet, however, still thought her a man, and did not in the least imagine that his companion was a beauty of the other sex.

Having passed an hour thus, Durat-el-Muluk could no longer conceal her love, and unveiled herself to see if Mehemet could discover that she was a lady. When Mehemet looked upon her, he thought he had never beheld such beauty, and mentally exclaimed, "O God, is there anything more beautiful in the world. If he were only a lady, would not every one be in love with him?" Then Mehemet cast down his eyes, as if confused, and she asked, "Why do you cast down your eyes as if you were ashamed?" and went to embrace him. Mehemet, who thought her a man, drew back, and turning red with indignation, addressed her thus: "Are you not ashamed to wish to embrace a man like yourself? Do you take me for a girl?"—"No, no," replied she, smiling. "Do not be frightened; did you not buy the dream, and come to catch it?"—"Yes," replied Mehemet; "I bought the dream, but where is it?—is this the dream?" Then she said, "My friend, you have bought a dream which you will be delighted with."—"If this is the dream," replied Mehemet, "I don't want it, for I have no need of it. It is true that I paid five sheep to have it, but I don't care for that, as I wished to get rid of them, and consequently don't regret the loss." Then she asked him again if he did not wish to have the dream. "Yes; I wish to have it, if it is something good." And she answered, "Behold the dream!" and uncovered her bosom, white as marble, and took off her turban and let down her hair, entwined with gold and pearls.

Then he perceived that she was a beautiful young damsel, and cried, "Heavens! you are a woman!"—"Yes," said she, and related to him her whole story from beginning to end; adding, "It seems that it is your fate to possess me instead of my cousin, who deserted me. Could you have caught a more beautiful dream?" Then he was seized with the most ardent love towards her, and began to kiss her hands and her cheeks; but she, being very virtuous, cried, "Stop, Mehemet, I am not yet your wife: when we shall be married, that which is now blamable in you will be your right." Then she arose, and told him to mount, saying, "Let us hasten on, for if my father's people overtake us, we are lost both of us." So they got on horseback, and rode all day until they came towards evening to a village where they stopped, and where they were taken for two young officers. They passed the night in the village, and the next morning went on. Thus they travelled for seven days, riding all day, and stopping at night to rest in the villages. The seventh day they arrived at a large town, and went and lodged at a khan (an Oriental inn, where there are only unfurnished rooms,) as two young officers. They went and visited the town, and the princess said to Mehemet, "I am tired of wearing this man's dress, but I cannot change it while we are at this khan, for every one has seen me in this dress. Go now to another khan, and engage an apartment for you and your slave; we will then quit the town, and after I have changed my dress, we will go to the khan where you will hire the apartment."

Now Mehemet, as we have said, was very simple, for he had seen but little of the world; but Durat-el-Muluk, who was exceedingly clever—thanks to the instruction of the wise man Zirajjan—made up for all deficiencies by instructing him how to act on all occasions.

Mehemet set out and engaged the lodging at the khan, and returned. Then the princess told him to mount on horseback as if they were going to start, and after having paid the landlord and taken leave of him, they left the town and came to a desert place. Then Durat-el-Muluk took off her man's attire and dressed herself as a female slave; and they returned to the city, and repaired to the khan where Mehemet had hired the lodging. Before, they had been taken for two young officers; now, every one took them for a young officer and his slave.

The lodging in the khan consisted of three chambers: Mehemet occupied the outer, and made his harem of the inner one. Being thus installed, they took a good dinner, and Mehemet demanded of Durat-el-Muluk what he should do next. She answered, "You must go and seek a respectable man, advanced in years, and two witnesses, and invite them to dine in your apartment. When you are at table with them, you will say, 'I have a female slave I have bought, whom I wish to emancipate and marry; the money which I paid for her will be her dowry; I beg of you now to make out a contract of marriage.' As for me," added she, "I make you a present of what you will have to pay for me according to the law."

Then Mehemet went to the mosque, invited the *imam* and two witnesses, and gave them a good dinner in his apartment. When they had eaten he told them that he had a slave he wished to marry, and begged them to draw up a contract of marriage. The *imam* accordingly drew up the contract, and signed it; and the two witnesses having affixed their seals, went away.

After their departure, Durat-el-Muluk said to her husband, "Now you possess the dream, I hope you do not regret your five sheep." Then Mehemet smiled, and thought in reality that all that had passed was a dream. In short, the two lovers, now man and wife, were the happiest people in the world, and enjoyed complete felicity for a long time. But, however, one day, the princess Durat-el-Muluk said to her husband, "My dear husband, we must not stay long in this town, which is in the jurisdiction of my father, for I am sure my father has sought me in all parts of his kingdom; and as he has not been able to discover me, no doubt before long he will apply to Zirajjan the philosopher, who will know by his magic where I am. Let us go then to a country which does not belong to my father, for if we are in a foreign country my father will have no right to send and take us by force." Mehemet replied, "I beg of you to do whatever you think proper, and I will obey your orders."

Then she took some of the jewels she had with her, and told him to go and sell them, which he did immediately; and they put their luggage on their horses, mounted, and rode out of the town. Having come to a lonely place, she took off her garments and disguised herself again as a man; then they continued to travel as before, riding all day and resting at night in the villages. In this way they had an opportunity of seeing the country, and passed their time very agreeably. On their way, Durat-el-Muluk instructed Mehemet in all the learning of the wise, which she had acquired from the philosopher Zirajjan, so that she made him an accomplished prince.

Thus this young man, who had been in the greatest wretchedness, attained the highest pitch of happiness.

After this, can it be denied that, when fortune comes, the most ignorant man becomes the most clever, and whatever he does turns to his good; while, when misfortune comes, the man who thinks himself the most learned turns out the most ignorant, and all that he does profits not?

To return to the happy pair. They travelled until they left the dominions of King Hassan, the father of Durat-el-Muluk, and arrived at a town the capital of King Gulnar. This king was a powerful monarch, who had immense armies at his command, and whose kingdom was most flourishing, for he administered justice among his people, who were contented and happy under his equitable rule. He had a vizier of great wisdom and penetration, endowed with every quality which makes a great minister, called Mushir (the Great Counsellor), on account of the wise counsels he gave on all occasions. The king always followed his advice, and never departed from his counsel. The royal city was most magnificent. There were beautiful edifices, and several large rivers crossing the city, and magnificent gardens around it. It was situated on the shore of the great ocean, and overlooked several provinces where the voyager must travel four months to reach the frontier. When they came to this town they went and lodged at a khan, and every day they went out to walk in the town. Durat-el-Muluk was still dressed as a man, and she was greatly pleased with all she saw, and the beauty of the town; and she inquired about everything, and in particular about the king, and studied the manners and customs of the people, and gained their friendship.

One night, as they were sitting together, Durat-el-Muluk

said to her husband, "I am tired of this lodging; I should like us to have a palace to ourselves, fitted to our station."— "Do whatever you please," replied Mehemet. "I have a plan in my head," she answered; "I will reflect on it tonight, and to-morrow I will put it in execution."

In reality, the next day she rose early, dressed herself as a man, and went out. She endeavoured to discover who were for the king, who against him, and what persons had the greatest influence in the kingdom. Thus she learnt, among other things, that there was a neighbouring king called Fidous, a powerful monarch, who exercised great influence over King Gulnar, who feared him, and sent presents to him for fear of his attacking his kingdom. With this information the princess returned home, and, taking some of her jewels, went to the jewellers' bazaar, and sold them for a great price. Then she went to the slave market and bought two black and two white slaves, and sent them home to the khan where they were living.

Every one in the town took Mehemet for a person of quality, for Durat-el-Muluk had bought him the dress worn by the nobles, and when he was dressed he looked indeed like a prince; and she bought presents worthy of a king's acceptance, and, putting them in golden platters covered with stuffs of divers colours embroidered with gold and pearls, ordered the two slaves to carry them, and said to Mehemet, "You must go to King Gulnar, salute him with great respect, and, having kissed the ground before him, say, 'I beg of your majesty to deign to accept these presents from your humble servant.' He will, no doubt, receive you well, and ask your name, who you are, and from what country you come; and then you must say, 'I am the son of King

Fidous. In consequence of a quarrel which I had with my father, I have been obliged to leave my county, and have come, with my family, to ask your protection, and to live in your kingdom.' Now, when the king hears you, he will offer you a post at court, or the government of a province; but you will say, 'O great king, if I had wanted a place at court or the government of a province I should have re- mained in my own country with my father; but as my only wish is to pass my time pleasantly in retirement, I beg of your majesty to grant me a small village on the sea-coast where I may live secluded.' When you have obtained per- mission for this from the king, you will return to me and let me know.''

Mehemet answered that he was ready to do whatsoever she wished, and set out with two slaves to carry the presents.

When they came to the palace they were admitted into the audience chamber, where the king was sitting on his throne, surrounded by his viziers and the great men of the empire. Then Mehemet advanced respectfully, and having kissed the ground, arose and addressed the king in an eloquent speech, in which he requested his majesty to accept the pre- sents he brought with him, and concluded by praying for the prosperity and long life of his majesty.

The king received him with great condescension, and ordered a seat to be given him near his person, as he took him for a prince by his dress and appearance. During this time the two slaves having been holding the platters of gold before the king, the vizier came forward, and, lifting the stuff which covered them, revealed the magnificent presents Mehemet had brought.

At this sight the esteem of the king was increased towards

Mehemet, and he addressed him, saying, "Judging from your presents and your appearance, you must be a great prince. What country do you come from? what is your name? and how can I serve you?"

Mehemet answered, "My name is Mehemet; I am the son of King Fidous, but have had a difference with him, and have left his kingdom, and have come to put myself under your protection, and to live in your dominions."

At these words King Gulnar was startled, and welcomed Mehemet with great cordiality, saying that nothing could be more agreeable to him than his coming. "You will be here," said he, "as if you were in your father's kingdom, and the greatest respect shall be paid to your high rank."

The king and the vizier both thought what Mehemet said was true, and were eager to show him attention on account of his father.

King Gulnar offered him the post of vizier or the government of a province to support him; but Mehemet replied, "I do not want the office of vizier or the government of a province, my only wish being to live in retirement; but if your majesty will grant me a small spot on the sea-coast, I will build a residence for myself and family, and employ the inhabitants, and thus I will live under your protection."

The king replied, "My whole kingdom is at your service. I beg of you to accept whatever spot you may like as a present; all I ask of you is to come to my court every day to see me. But where are you living now?"

" At the khan," said Mehemet.

" It is not fit for a man of your rank to live in a khan," said the king; and, turning to one of his viziers, he ordered him to have a palace prepared for Mehemet immediately.

A palace was accordingly prepared, and furnished fit for the reception of a prince.

Then Mehemet returned to Durat-et-Muluk, and recounted to her all that had happened.

Immediately she arose, dressed herself as a man, and repaired to the palace, where she was delighted with all she saw, and at her return, expressed her satisfaction to Mehemet.

King Gulnar ordered, according to the custom in the East, for them to be provided with provisions, and every necessary for them and their suite.

Then the princess Durat-el-Muluk said to Mehemet, "To-morrow we will ride out and choose an agreeable spot for our residence."

Mehemet consented, and accordingly, the next day, having bought four horses for the slaves, she dressed herself as a man, and mounted with Mehemet, and, the four slaves following behind, they left the town.

Having come to the sea-coast, they saw a ruined village in a spot which the princess thought would suit them. When they returned home, Durat-el-Muluk said to her husband, "To-morrow you will go to the king, and say I have chosen such a village. If the king should remark, it is in ruins, you will say, it does not matter, and that you will rebuild it. At the same time you will request him to send for the pro-prietors to sell the ground, and then you will buy the ground, and afterwards return home, and relate all that has occurred to me."

The next morning Mehemet went to the divan, and the

king received him most graciously, and asked him if he had selected a spot for his residence.

Mehemet replied that he had chosen the ruined village on the sea-coast.

The king said that he ought to have selected a better place, and not a ruined village; but Mehemet said that if the king would allow him, he would buy it and rebuild it, and for that purpose he begged him to send for the proprietors, that he might agree with them.

Thereupon, the king ordered it to be proclaimed in the streets by the crier, that whoever possessed land in that village should come before him; and when all the proprietors had come, he commanded them to sell their land to Mehemet; and Mehemet bought the whole village, and received the documents of the sale. The king, however, would not allow Mehemet to pay, but paid the whole price himself.

The king showed all this favour to Mehemet out of consideration for his pretended father.

Mehemet returned to Durat-el-Muluk, and related all that had passed to her, and she was delighted. She told Mehemet to send for the chief of the architects, whom the king had commanded to obey the instructions of Mehemet; and when he arrived, Mehemet made a contract with him to build a village and a palace, such as had never been seen, and paid him his money in advance.

The architect immediately set about building the village and the palace, and soon both were finished to their entire satisfaction.

The princess Durat-el-Muluk sent furniture and everything necessary to the palace, so that all was ready in less than three months.

When all was done, Mehemet said to Durat-el-Muluk, "The palace is finished, it is true, but I fear that we shall soon be discovered, and pay dearly for our boldness."

Durat-el-Muluk answered, "How can we be discovered? The king Fidous, whose son you said you were, lives six months' journey from here, and news cannot arrive from there in less time than that, so your fears are groundless. As for me, I am not satisfied with what I have done for you, and I hope to see you one day the king of this country, if you will have patience and keep quiet."

"How can I be the king of this country?" said Mehemet. "It is true we have built a village, but we have no inhabitants; and how can we live in a place where there are no people?"

"We have not finished yet," answered she. "To-morrow morning you will go to the court, and beg the king Gulnar to send for the proprietors of the ground, and when they come you will give them back their documents, and say that you make them a present of the ground they sold you, and although all was in ruins when they sold it you, you have great pleasure to say that a well-built village now awaits them. You will then invite them to come and live there, and promise to give them money to cultivate the ground with. Thus, they will return to the village, and its people will be devoted to you ever after."

In reality, the next morning, Mehemet went to the court, and did as the princess Durat-el-Muluk directed.

When all the proprietors of the village were assembled, Mehemet gave them back the documents, made them a present of the land, and promised them money to enable them to cultivate it.

The people of the place were overjoyed at this proposal, and thanked Mehemet warmly; and the king also thought his conduct most laudable, and expressed his approbation of it to him.

Soon afterwards the people went in crowds to inhabit the village, and commenced cultivating the land and planting gardens. Thus the village which had been a heap of ruins and the den of wild beasts became an earthly paradise.

The princess Durat-el-Muluk bought slaves of both sexes, and, having had everything carried to the new palace, removed there with her husband, and they took up their abode there.

The news was soon spread that the son of King Fidous had come and built a village, which they called the "Village of Fidous," and visitors and the curious flocked from all parts to see it.

Mehemet received all who came to the village with great kindness, and treated them most hospitably; so that he gained their friendship, and his fame spread throughout all countries.

This, however, did not prevent him from going every day to the court.

The revenue of the village increased every day, and Mehemet employed it all in building new houses, bazaars, mosques, baths, and schools.

Thus the village became a small city, and Mehemet, who was really the king, had a throne put at the gate of his palace and judged the people. He had his ministers, public officers, and all the officials which are to be found in a great court.

In all cases of dispute the inhabitants had recourse to him, and never failed to be satisfied with his decision.

All the inhabitants of the empire came in crowds to see the new city, to admire its palaces, gardens, and public fountains; so that the little city of Fidous became the garden of the empire, and the resort of the whole population.

Now the king Gulnar had two musicians, one of whom played on the harp and the other on the lute, distinguished no less by their musical talents than by their powers of diverting by their improvised poetry and witty remarks. They were not only the favourites of the king, but were invited by all the great men of the capital to solace them with the sound of their beautiful voices and skilful playing.

One day, one of the musicians said to his companion, "Let us go and visit King Mehemet, son of King Fidous, in his little city, and divert him by our music; we are sure to be well paid for our trouble, by what I hear." So, the same day, they took their instruments, left the town, and set out for the so-called "City of the son of King Fidous."

When they arrived there, they visited all the sights of the town; and, going from place to place, came at last to the gate of the palace of Mehemet, and entered the court. Mehemet observing them, made a sign for them to ascend to the saloon where he was sitting; and they ascended, and saluted him respectfully. Mehemet, on his part, received them most graciously, and ordered them to be shown all the palace; after which they were conducted into a chamber, where there was a table spread with a splendid repast.

Having eaten, they returned before Mehemet, and begged him to give them permission to play to him, telling him they were the musicians to the king and to the great men of the empire.

Mehemet replied that nothing would give him greater pleasure.

So the servants brought them their instruments, which they had left at the gate of the palace; and they played, and Mehemet's soul was delighted.

The princess Durat-el-Muluk, hearing the music, looked from behind the curtain, and was enchanted with the melody of their voices.

Such is the character of woman; let her be the most retired, she cannot resist the temptation to listen, and look out when she hears the voice of a stranger.

Now, when the two musicians saw Durat-el-Muluk, they thought they saw the moon rising from behind the clouds, for such was her beauty that no one could behold her without being struck with it; and their joy at seeing so much loveliness increased until they were mad with delight. Mehemet, however, did not notice this circumstance, and when they had finished, he took a handful of gold, and gave it them; and they thanked him, and returned to the city, delighted with their adventure.

Now it so happened, that twice during the absence of the musicians, fate willed it that the king should send for them, and the servants returned saying that they were not to be found. The third time, however, the servants finding them at home, brought them before the king. The king, who had been expecting them a long time, asked them where they had been so long; and they told him they had paid a visit to Mehemet, the son of King Fidous, and that they had seen his little city, and played before him.

Then the king asked them if he had acted generously towards them. "Yes, indeed," said they; "he not only gave us a splendid repast, but a handful of gold;" and they began to sing his praise.

"Has he fine horses and a great suite?" asked the king.

"Yes, your majesty, he has the finest horses, beautifully caparisoned, and slaves and servants in splendid liveries; but what we most admired was a lady of surpassing beauty, who is his wife or slave, and whose beauty is such that when we saw her we were mad and drunk without wine;" and hereupon they began to eulogize her in the highest terms.

Upon this King Gulnar, who loved beautiful women, fell in love with the princess Durat-el-Muluk without seeing her, from their report. When the music was finished he gave a present to the musicians and dismissed them, and entered his chamber; but he could do nothing but think of the princess Durat-el-Muluk, and became more and more in love with her every hour. At last his passion grew so violent that he could resist it no longer; he would have given worlds to know whether she were the slave or wife of Mehemet; and as he did not know how to find out this, he was in the greatest perplexity.

He entered his audience chamber and sent for the vizier Mushir, and when he came, took him apart and spoke to him thus: "My dear Mushir, you know that a good vizier ought always to give good counsel, and that when a king is in a critical position, it is for his minister to extricate him by his ability and experience."

"O king of the age," answered the vizier, "I am your most obedient servant. What has happened? Has your majesty heard that some king is about to attack the kingdom?"

"No, no," replied the king; "if it were an affair of war we

could have remedied it by men and money; but it is an affair of the heart, and a malady of the heart must be treated by a skilful physician."

"I beg your majesty to explain," said the vizier; and "I will do my utmost to find a remedy."

Then the king related to him all that the musicians had told him, and how they had been at the city of Mehemet, son of King Fidous, and concluded by saying, "They say they have seen a lady of such unequalled beauty, that when they described her to me I fell in love with her from their report. I have done all I could to forget her, but my heart is filled with her love. I know not whether she be his slave, wife, or concubine; but the fire of love continues to increase in my heart, and I cannot be cured of my malady but by possessing her. I beg of you, therefore, to find some means by which I may obtain her, for you are a man of experience and ability, and I have confidence in you."

When the vizier heard these words he was plunged in a sea of thought, and all the more perplexed as he loved Mehemet sincerely. So he began to comfort the king, but proposed no plan, until, seeing this produced quite a contrary effect to that which he wished, he said, "It is an easy thing, your majesty; I will not fail to find a plan; but, first of all, I must know whether she be his wife or his slave: for that purpose I will send immediately an old woman to make inquiry. If the beauty be his slave, we will offer a great sum to obtain her, and, as he is the son of a king, and naturally generous, he will not refuse her to us; but if she be his wife, I know of no plan, and I hope your majesty will endeavour to resist your passion."

The king answered, "I beg of you to send immediately,

for I cannot resist my feelings, and am impatient to possess her."

So the vizier arose and left the king, went and spoke to an old servant of the palace, and told her to go to the city of Mehemet, son of King Fidous, and, under the pretence of visiting his palace, to inquire if the beautiful lady were his wife or his slave, and bring him the news as soon as possible.

The old woman set out, and went to the city of Mehemet, and gained admission to the apartments of Durat-el-Muluk, who received her with great kindness, as she took her for a midwife. On her part, the old woman behaved with great, respect, but asked a great number of questions. Among other things, she asked if the prince were her husband. The princess answered that he was her husband, but that he had quarrelled with his father, and in consequence they had been obliged to leave their country and live in a foreign land.

The old woman consoled Durat-el-Muluk, saying she hoped she would return one day to her native land and home; then saluted her and took her leave, and went immediately to the vizier, and told him that the beautiful lady was the wife of Mehemet, and that the others were but his slaves. Then the vizier understood in what a critical position he was, for he knew how obstinate the king was in his desires; however, he went to him, and represented to him, with the greatest humility, what had happened, saying, "I have to inform your majesty that, according to the information I have received, the beautiful lady is the wife and cousin of Mehemet, and neither his slave nor his concubine. I, therefore, entreat your majesty most respectfully to resist the temptation of Satan, and not allow your heart to be overcome by a passion which is justifiable neither before God nor man."

When the king heard this he replied, "I insist that you find a plan to obtain the object of my love, for I am vanquished by my passion, and cannot resist, and fear that I shall commit some rash act."

The vizier answered, "I beg your majesty to consider that it is out of my power to give advice in an affair which offends God, and which will bring great misfortune upon us. You cannot ignore that it is forbidden, according to the law of the Prophet, to take the wife of another man until after his death, or until he has divorced her. I know, therefore, of no plan."

The king answered, "I will find a plan myself: I will have her husband killed and take her."

Then the vizier answered, "You have no right, and it is not your interest to kill him. Your majesty is aware that everybody knows that he came to ask your hospitality, and to put himself under your protection. If the report of his murder be spread, you will meet with nothing but opprobrium from all the sultans and kings of the earth, and your name will become a by-word amongst them. They will say, 'This is the man, who, to gratify his passion, sacrificed his honour.' Besides, I must tell your majesty, it is a grave affair, and very perilous; for if his father, Fidous, discover that you have killed his son, he will come upon us with a great army, raze our town to the ground, and devastate the whole country. Your majesty knows that we are not strong enough to resist King Fidous; and thus this unhappy passion, if you give way to it, will lead to the ruin and downfall of the empire."

When the king heard the words of the vizier, he was

greatly frightened, feeling the full force of what he said. However, he concealed his project, and passed the whole of the night without sleeping, such was the violence of his passion.

The next morning he sent again to the vizier Mushir, and told him that he had passed a sleepless night, and could neither eat nor drink; and added, that his passion grew stronger and stronger, and entreated him to find some cure for his malady.

The vizier again endeavoured to dissuade him from his project by every argument possible, but in vain; they produced no effect on the king, who, seeing he could get nothing from Mushir, went to another vizier called Jaifoul, communicated his secret to him, and, telling him the whole affair from beginning to end, begged of him to find out some way to help him.

This vizier, who was very imprudent, and did not consider the consequences of a thing before doing it, said to the king, "There is nothing easier in the world than to obtain the object of your wishes; as king of this country, you have only to send and have Mehemet killed, for no one dare oppose your will."—"That will not do," answered the king; "for your colleague, Mushir, has shown me the consequences of such an act; and I think he is right, for, if I have Mehemet killed, his father will come and take vengeance on me." And he explained to him all that Mushir had said.

Then the vizier Jaifoul answered, "That is true, but I have another plan: we will have him killed by another without compromising ourselves. Your majesty knows that in the 'Island,' which is on the limits of your kingdom, there lives one of the genii, who, during your father's lifetime, was

long the scourge of the country—who stopped travellers on the
road, or carried them off and devoured them, and committed
all kinds of ravages in that part of the country. Your father,
incensed by these ravages beyond all endurance, endeavoured
to find a remedy, and assembled all the magicians of the
empire, and told them to put a stop to the outrage committed
by the genius. So one of the magicians enchanted him, and
confined him in that isle, and now he can do whatever he
pleases there, but cannot cross to the continent. If you wish,·
therefore, to get rid of Mehemet, you have only to send for
him, do him great honour, and tell him that you know the
valour of his father and how he inherits it; and that as there
is a rebel on the confines of your dominion, who stops the
roads, you wish him to go at the head of a division to kill or
take him. Now, as the young man is of great courage, and
you will not tell him that the rebel is one of the genii, he will
be sure to accept the command. At the same time you will tell
the troops when they arrive at the island, to let Mehemet go
on, and to remain behind. When he is once there, the giant
will not fail to rush on him and devour him, and your troops
not having passed the boundary of the enchanted isle, will
return in safety. Thus you may get rid of Mehemet without
compromising yourself, and then you can take his wife; and as
no doubt his father will soon hear of his death, you will send
and tell him that his son fell in battle, and send him presents
to calm him; for with presents you can do anything."

King Gulnar was delighted with this plan, and thanked his
vizier Jaifoul, and rewarded him bountifully for it.

The next morning he sent for Mehemet, and when he came
he did him great honour, and made him sit near him, and
having had coffee and the pipe presented to him, said,

"My dear Mehemet, your father is distinguished in the world
by his valour, and I know that you are no less brave than
he.   Now, I have just heard that a rebel has appeared on the
boundary of my kingdom—a great robber, who infests the
roads and stops travellers.   Now, as I have the greatest confidence in your courage, I want you to go with a troop of
soldiers to kill or take this fellow prisoner."

When Mehemet heard this proposal of the king, he
answered, "Obedience to your majesty is before all things
to me.   I will get ready this very day, and to-morrow will
put myself at the head of the troop and set out, and I will
not return except with this fellow, dead or alive."

The king was greatly delighted at this, and thanked
Mehemet warmly.

Then Mehemet went to his palace and to Durat-el-Muluk,
and related to her all the king had said to him.   She
immediately prepared her instruments of magic to discover
who and where the rebel was; and found that he was a terrible
genius, who devoured men as men do shrimps. She was in the
greatest perplexity at this discovery, and knew not what to
do ; for she was aware that if they were to fly, King Gulnar
would send his horsemen and pursue and catch them ; and if
her husband were to accept the commission, he would fall a
victim.   Having reflected for a long time, she at last recol-
lected her friend Badr-el-Maha, with whom she had studied
philosophy and magic under the wise man Zirajjan; and
knowing that Badr-el-Maha was very skilful in discovering
treasures and breaking talismans, she bethought herself of
asking her assistance, for she had discovered by her instruments of magic that the great giant could only be killed by
a certain enchanted sabre, hidden in one of the treasures of

the wise men of olden times, in a great mountain in the centre of Africa, without which no one could kill this giant.

Now Durat-el-Muluk was very skilful in the science of magic, but still she could not break the talisman, nor discover the treasure, and she knew that Badr-el-Maha excelled particularly in that science.

So she took her instruments to discover in what part of the world Badr-el-Maha was, and found that she had retired to a palace in the midst of the desert, which she had had built by aid of her servants the genii, and where she lived apart from the world.

The reader knows that Durat-el-Muluk, Badr-el-Maha, and Nuzhat-ez-Zeman, were all three educated by the philosopher Zirajjan, and that when the father of Durat-el-Muluk sent to fetch her, her companions felt the greatest grief at her departure.

Now, twelve months after this, the father of Badr-el-Maha sent to fetch his daughter, who, as we have said, excelled in the knowledge of talismans. Unfortunately, a short after her father died, and his son, her brother, succeeded him; and as Badr-el-Maha loved her father tenderly, she was greatly afflicted at his death, and said to the king her brother, "My dear brother, after the death of my beloved father I cannot remain in the country, and will go abroad to forget my grief." Her brother, who loved her greatly, did not wish to disappoint her, and said to her, "My dear sister, do what you please; but your separation from me will cause me great pain." But she answered, "I wish to go and choose a spot in the desert, where I can build a palace in which I can live in retirement; and, although I shall be at a great distance, I will not fail to come and see you from time to time. I will always watch over your welfare, and evil be to him who tries to injure you, for I will infallibly ruin him by the aid of the genii who are in my service."

Thereupon she took leave of her brother, mounted into her balloon, and sailed away into the air. Having visited many countries, she at last selected a well-watered spot, with a delightful climate, in a picturesque neighbourhood, and commanded the genii to build a high palace there, and lived in retirement, served by the genii, devoting herself exclusively to the study of magic and the knowledge of talismans; however, she did not fail to go from time to time to visit her brother.

Durat-el-Muluk also discovered that her palace was in Upper China. So she took courage and said to Mehemet, "Fear not, for you are about to obtain the object of your wishes. All you have to do is to go to-morrow to King Gulnar, and say to him that you beg of him to allow you to go alone, without any guard; for as the rebel is but one man, you feel confidence enough to go and attack him alone, and are sure that you will take him dead or alive, if even he should be the greatest of the genii, if he will only grant you the space of twenty days to go and return. Then you will come to me, and I will tell you what is necessary to be done."

The next morning accordingly Mehemet repaired to the king.

The king, in the meantime, had prepared a troop whom he had confidence in, and told them not to pass the boundary of the enchanted isle, but to let Mehemet cross alone, and be devoured by the genii, and then to return to him and keep the secret.

When Mehemet presented himself before the king, the king asked him if he had made his preparations; and Mehemet replied that he was quite ready to go, but that he begged of his majesty to let him go alone, and that should the rebel be the greatest of the genii, he would not fail to bring him, dead or alive.

This proposal caused the king great joy, for he was sure Mehemet would never return, and therefore was prodigal in his thanks and praises to him.

Mehemet asked him to grant him a certain number of days to execute his mission in; and the king having answered that the rebel was seven days' journey off, Mehemet asked seven to go, seven to return, and six for the combat—in all twenty days. The king granted him this request, glad to obtain his wish so easily, and loaded with presents the vizier who had suggested this plan to him.

As for the vizier Mushir, he was greatly pained, and said to himself, "Alas, alas! the young man is lost, no doubt;" but he dared not speak out, for fear of the king.

Mehemet returned to Durat-el-Muluk, and related to her all that had taken place, and she replied, "Very good; everything in the world has a cause and effect. As for the cause of this, we know very well what is the cause of the king's acting in this way; as for the effect, we shall see what effect such conduct will produce. However, we must not lose time, and must have courage. Now, take this letter, get on horseback, and follow the road that your horse takes, and rest where he will stop at the approach of night. As for the provisions you will need, you will find enough of them in a valise, which is on the horse's back, to last you till you reach the palace of Badr-el-Maha, when you will call out to the

inhabitants of the palace, and a young damsel of surpassing
beauty will open a window and ask you what you want.
Then you will show her the letter, salute her most respectfully, and tell her you have brought a letter from one of her
best friends, and that you cannot return without the answer.
In the meantime, while you wait for the answer, you will do
whatever she orders."   •

Mehemet sprang on horseback, and Durat-el-Muluk fixed a
talisman on the horse's neck, and said, "May your return be
happy." Then Mehemet asked, "But in what direction must
I go?" Durat-el-Muluk answered, "Leave the bridle to
the horse;" and Mehemet let go the bridle, and set out.

Having travelled all day, and passed through many cities
without stopping, towards evening the horse halted near a
village, at the foot of a tree by which there ran a spring.

Then Mehemet alighted, spread his carpet on the grass,
and fed and watered his horse; and that done, performed his
ablutions and began to eat. He passed the night in that
spot, and early the next morning mounted on horseback, and
continued his journey thus for ten days.

The eleventh day he discovered a beautiful palace, and
when he arrived beneath the windows he cried out as Durat-el-Muluk had commanded him, "O inhabitants of this
palace!" Badr-el-Maha, who had not seen a man since her
arrival at the palace, was greatly astonished when she heard
his voice, and opening the window and seeing a fine young
man on horseback, asked what he wanted. Mehemet replied,
"Madam, I bring you a letter, and await the answer." Then
Badr-el-Maha ordered one of the genii in the form of a man
to open the gate; and the genius who served as porter opened
the gate, and held the stirrup for Mehemet while he alighted,

led his horse to the stable of the palace, and brought him before Badr-el-Maha.

When Mehemet came before her he was greatly surprised at her beauty, and she was no less surprised to see so handsome a young man. Then she arose and received him most graciously on account of his beauty, and made him sit near her, and asked the cause that had brought him to her.

Mehemet presented the letter to her, saying, "That letter will let you know, madam, for what motive I have come to you, and I beg of you therefore to read it."

Badr-el-Maha took the letter, and found it ran thus :—

" From Durat-el-Muluk, to her beloved sister Badr-el-Maha, with her salutation and compliments.

" The bearer of this is my cousin and friend. It is unnecessary for me at present to state any further particulars, than that we are now in the country of King Gulnar, and that the king has desired my cousin, the light of my eyes, as a pretext for his destruction, to kill the ' Giant of the Island.'

" Now, I beg of you to give us your help in this affair, for I have discovered, by what knowledge I have in the science of geomancy, that this giant is only to be vanquished by help of the enchanted sword in one of the caves of the ' Treasures of the Wise,' in the rocky valley of the burning mountain ; and as I know that you are deeply versed in the science of discovering treasures, and can aid us if you will, I beseech you to enable this youth to obtain this sword ; and then, when he has returned in safety, may you leave your solitary abode, and come and dwell with us, and let us live together under the same roof again, as we often wished we might, when with the philosopher Zirajjan."

Now, when Badr-el-Maha read the letter and understood

its meaning, and saw the mysterious working of predestination in the affair, she rejoiced greatly, and welcomed Mehemet with great warmth; and when morning came, she mounted her balloon and bade Mehemet mount after her, and she touched a spring, and the balloon flew off with them up into the air, and before long they came to a mountain, and Badr-el-Maha alighted.

Then she kindled a fire and spoke some cabalistic words, and the mountain opened and revealed an iron door, inlaid with sheets of brass; and she pressed a spring, and the door opened, but in the entrance were volumes of smoke barring the way to all comers.

Then Badr-el-Maha spoke some few words and the smoke disappeared, and she said to Mehemet, "Come, follow me, and take this censer, and fear not whatsoever thou mayest see."

Then Mehemet took the censer and walked behind her, and they passed through the doorway. And lo! they beheld a machine formed of revolving swords, terrific to look on; and Badr-el-Maha touched a brazen knob, and a trap opened in the ground and discovered a subterranean passage filled with wheels and screws, and all kinds of machinery, working a single chain connected with the door, the chain being fastened to a pillar of gold supporting the door connected with the wheels and screws on the right and left.

Then Badr-el-Maha cut the chain, and immediately the whole of the machinery stopped, and they passed on to a second door of iron, which opened of itself, and then to a third of brass; but when they came to the fourth, Badr-el-Maha stopped, for, be it known, that in this doorway there was a machine so cunningly contrived, that when the door was opened, a chain fastened to it and communicating with the machine, caused a discharge of vitriol on whomsoever entered.

Now, Badr-el-Maha, being aware of this stratagem, signed to Mehemet to draw back, and, keeping her body carefully hidden by the door itself, drew the door back so that the vitriol fell harmless in the doorway. Then they passed on and came to a fifth door, connected with which was an equally cunning device, by which, when the door was opened, an arrow was discharged through the doorway. This also Badr-el-Maha and Mehemet succeeded in passing in safety, and came at last to the treasure-chambers. Here gold, silver, and precious stones lay heaped on all sides in such profusion as to dazzle the eye; and it was to guard these treasures, collected by the wise men of olden times, that they had contrived all the devices we have spoken of. Here they had accumulated their treasures from age to age, thinking no one would ever be sufficiently versed in science to discover them. But, as we have said, Badr-el-Maha had, by the aid of the philosopher Zirajjan, become most expert in the science of discovering treasures, and hence had been enabled to discover the locality of the so-called "Treasures of the Wise," and to penetrate thus far.

When Badr-el-Maha, with Mehemet after her, had entered, she moved to the centre of the chamber, where was a smith's forge of clay, near a square column, to which, high up, was suspended a chest. And lo! when Badr-el-Maha approached, the chest descended on the forge, into her very hands, and she opened it, and drew forth a sword made of seven metals and talismans, and took it, and said to Mehemet, "Arise, let us be gone."

And Mehemet said, "And these jewels and precious stones; shall we not take some of them?"

And Badr-el-Maha replied, "They are not ours, and there is nothing for us here but this sword, and nothing that we want but it."

Then she left the treasure-chamber, and they returned as they had come; and, behold, all was restored as it was before —the mountain, and all that was in it.

When they regained the open air, they sat down, and ate and drank; and Badr-el-Maha said to Mehemet, "O Mehemet, now that I have done so much for thee, thou wilt surely marry me."

And said Mehemet, "So would I fain do, but I am married to my cousin, Durat-el-Muluk."

"That matters not," answered Badr-el-Maha; "for we have always been sisters, and desired to live under the same roof: but now, however, you must go and kill the giant, and then I will return with thee to Durat-el-Muluk."

So she arose, and mounted into the balloon, and Mehemet with her, and they traversed the air until they came to her palace. When they arrived there, Mehemet rested one day, and the next morning Badr-el-Maha provided him with the necessaries for his journey, and told him to ascend into the balloon, and commanded the genii her servants to carry him whithersoever he wished. And they replied, "To hear is to obey." Then they departed, and travelled until they came to the island inhabited by the giant.

Now this island was on the sea-coast, and thickly covered with trees and vegetation, and only separated from the shore by a narrow arm of the sea.

In olden times the giant had not confined his devastations

to the island, but had infested the roads of the provinces in the adjacent part of the empire, laying everything waste that came in his way, and devouring the children and young maidens ; but in the reign of King Gulnar a great astrologer and magician had succeeded in confining this monster to the island, by causing sheets of flame to stop his passage whenever he attempted to cross to the main land.

Such was the state of things, then, when Mehemet arrived —no traveller or merchant daring to cross over to the island, and the passage that way completely stopped, the island left entirely to the giant, and inhabited only by himself and the wild beasts. Such, at least, is the account we have of it from the historians of that time.

Now when Mehemet and Badr-el-Maha came to the island, and the monster saw the balloon, and Mehemet and Badr-el-Maha in it, he arose ready to seize them.

Then Badr-el-Maha said to Mehemet, " Quick now, shake the sword in the giant's face."

And, behold, as soon as Mehemet shook the sword in the giant's face, the giant fell motionless, and as if dead, to the ground.

"Go now," said Badr-el-Maha, "and destroy him with the sword, and fear not, for he is incapable of moving."

Then Mehemet approached the prostrate monster with a bold heart, and slew him, and cut off his head; and they remounted into the balloon, taking the head of the giant with them.

Thus they travelled, making for the country of King Gulnar, until they arrived, at midnight, at the palace of Durat-el-Muluk.

Then Mehemet alighted, and entered the apartments of

Durat-el-Muluk, and she saluted him and embraced him, and asked what had happened to him; and he related all that had occurred, and what Badr-el-Maha had said.

During this time Badr-el-Maha had remained waiting on the house-top; but no sooner did Durat-el-Muluk hear of her being there than she went out to meet her, and welcomed her to the palace.

Then Badr-el-Maha inquired how she had come to live in that country, and Durat-el-Muluk informed her of every thing, and she marvelled greatly at her strange history.

So they retired to rest; and the next day there remained but four days to the expiration of the time by which Mehemet was to return to the king.

Then Durat-el-Muluk urged that her sister Badr-el-Maha should be united to Mehemet without loss of time; and so they sent for the witnesses, and drew up the contract of marriage, and Badr-el-Maha was legally married to Mehemet.

The next day Mehemet proposed to go and lay the monster's head before the king; but Badr-el-Maha would not let him depart, saying, "It is not yet necessary to go, and why leave me so soon?" So Mehemet acceded to her wishes, and tarried yet some time longer at the palace; and the inhabitants of the village, high and low, assembled, and there was feasting and rejoicing for many days.

But to return to the treacherous King Gulnar. The day on which Mehemet had departed, he sent for his viziers, and said to them, "I will send and have the wife of this fellow brought to me, for we know very well he will never come back."

Then said the vizier Mushir, "O king, have patience until the term appointed be complete, and give not the people

cause to blame you. Wait only some twenty days after the
appointed time, and the news of his death must arrive, and
then you can take his wife with impunity. Should we be
asked concerning how he came to go, we can say that, as we
were conversing one day, we happened to speak about this
monster, and what ravages he committed in that part of your
majesty's dominions, when Mehemet offered to go and bring
the rebel's head and lay it at your feet, and persisted in
going, spite of all we could say to dissuade him." Thus the
vizier Mushir counselled the king, and succeeded in making
him wait until the day before that on which the term given
would expire. On the morning of this day, Badr-el-Maha
said to Mehemet, "Arise, O Mehemet! and take the head to
the king." And she put the head in a dish of gold, and said
to her genii, "Carry this head, and go before your master ;"
and they replied only by saying, "To hear is to obey."

Now when Mehemet approached, some slaves ran and
informed King Gulnar, saying, "Behold, Mehemet, the son
of King Fidous, is approaching."

When King Gulnar heard these words, his senses left him,
and he knew not what he did. Mehemet, in the meantime,
had come to the palace, and entered the divan, followed by
the genii bearing the monster's head, and saluted the king,
and knelt before him, and presented the giant's head. The
king, however, could not say a word, for his tongue clove to
his mouth with wonder.

So the vizier Mushir stepped forward and welcomed
Mehemet, and congratulated him ; and, in the meantime, the
king, having somewhat recovered, thanked Mehemet, and
ordered him a dress of honour, and Mehemet stayed some

E

few days, and then asked permission to depart, and returned to his city, to Durat-el-Muluk and Badr-el-Maha.

As soon as Mehemet had left, King Gulnar turned to his viziers, and said to them, "Now what think you of this business? We sent this fellow to destruction, as we thought, and he returns triumphant, and has killed the monster. Who could have imagined such a thing!"

Then said the vizier Mushir, "Did I not counsel you at first, O king, not to interfere with this youth, for that he was protected by Fate, and was the favourite of Fortune? How else could he have escaped this danger, and killed the giant who was the scourge of that part of the country? My only fear now is, that he should discover the plot that was laid for him, and take vengeance on your majesty; and so I would advise you to send him on a pilgrimage, and to make no further attempt on his life."

Then the king sat silent, and could think of naught but the beauty of Mehemet's wife, and neglected all business.

Mehemet, in the meantime, had returned to his palace, to the agreeable society of the two princesses, with whom he passed his days in unbroken and unalloyed happiness.

His fame, in the meanwhile, had spread throughout the surrounding country, and the tale of his having killed the giant was in every man's mouth.

One day, as he was sitting thus in his palace, the musicians of the king again visited him, and he received them with great honour, and regaled them.

Then they struck their instruments and began to play, and Badr-el-Maha, who was in the inner apartment, moved back the curtain to look out and see what it was, and discovered herself and Durat-el-Muluk, who was sitting with

her. The musicians, amazed at the dazzling beauty of the
young princesses, were near losing their senses in the excess
of their admiration, and could only compare the princesses to
the sun and moon in beauty; and they redoubled their efforts,
stimulated by this sight, and surpassed themselves in their
performance; and Mehemet spared not his gold, but rewarded
them munificently, and they returned to the capital singing
the praises of Mehemet and the princesses.

Some days after their return, the king sent for them to
play before him, and, during the conversation, the name of
Mehemet being mentioned in connexion with his killing the
giant, the musicians related how they had been to Mehemet,
and how sumptuously he had regaled them, expatiating greatly
on the beauty of another lady whom they had seen at his
palace, whom he had brought back with him from his
journey, and who even excelled the first in loveliness.

Now when the king heard this, he was nearly beside himself with envy, and the fire of jealousy was kindled in his
heart; and he sent for his vizier Mushir, and informed him
of what he had heard, and said, "I will wait no longer,
but will have this man killed."

The vizier answered, "O king, I will have naught to do
in such an affair. Behold, I have told you that this youth is
under the especial protection of Fate, and that whatever evil
is sought to be done him, will only recoil on his enemies."

Then the king sent for his other viziers, and explained the
affair to them; and one of them said, "Surely, no one would
have thought that he would have returned from the errand
we sent him on safe and sound, as he has done; but there
still remains one way by which we may be rid of him."

The king inquired what it was, and the vizier answered,

" We must send him to fetch some apples from the ' Garden of the Philosophers,' for you must know that that garden is inhabited only by young maidens, and if any man enter, he is immediately deprived of motion, and slain by them; so, should he consent to go to make the rash attempt, he must infallibly perish. This is the plan I propose, O king, to rid us of this fellow."

Then answered the king, " Surely, I will do this, and thou hast spoken wisely; haste and send for Mehemet."

So the vizier sent a courier after Mehemet; and he came to Mehemet at his castle, and kissed the ground before him and saluted him, and said, " O prince, know that the king, my master, has need of thee, and requires thy presence near his person, and requests thee to come with all speed, for he has to confer with thee on an affair of grave moment."

Then Durat-el-Muluk consulted her instruments of magic, and discovered the motive of the king, and that he wished only to send Mehemet to destruction ; but she said to Mehemet, " The king desires only thy death, but go to him and hear what he says, and then return, and inform me of it."

So Mehemet arose and went to the king, and the king received him with great cordiality, and feasted him; and when they had eaten, the vizier said to Mehemet, " You must know that the king wants you to do him a service, but is ashamed to ask it of you."

" What is the service ?" asked Mehemet.

The vizier said, " The king has a daughter who is grievously sick, and near unto death, whom the physicians say nothing can save but eating of the apples of the ' Garden of the Philosophers.' Now the service which the king would ask of you is, to go and fetch some of these apples, that his daughter

may not die; but he hesitates to ask this of you, as there is
great danger and peril to be faced in obtaining them, and so
said to me, 'O vizier, I am ashamed to take advantage of the
kindness of this stranger in our land, so speak you to him,
and tell him what has befallen me.' And I answered, 'I will
inform him, O king;' and, behold, I have informed you, and
I know from thy goodness that thou wilt help the king, and
do your utmost for his sake. May God reward and repay you
for it."

When Mehemet heard this, he replied, "To hear is to obey.
This affair is the easiest thing possible; and even if it were
necessary to expend my soul for his majesty, it would be my
duty to do it, rather than that he should want the least
thing."

The vizier said, "Blame me not then if evil befall thee, for
I have told thee danger awaits thee."

Then Mehemet arose, and, behold, neither he nor the vizier,
nor the king, knew where the garden was, except by hearsay;
and he came to his city, and to his wives, and informed them
of what the king demanded of him.

Then said Durat-el-Muluk, "I leave this affair to my sister
Badr-el-Maha, for she understands calendars, and is expert in
such matters as this."

So Badr-el-Maha arose, and examined into the affair by the
aid of her magic science, and found that the king wished only
to kill Mehemet.

She immediately went out and prepared the balloon, and
told Mehemet to mount into it, saying, "Go whithersoever
this take you, and descend there, for it will stop over the
'Garden of the Philosophers;' enter the garden, and you
will see there a large marble basin of water, and around this

seats.   Then hide yourself under the highest of these seats,
and you will see a flight of birds come, and light each on a
seat, and they will take off their clothes of feathers and come
forth young maidens, and go down into the water.   Then go
and take the dress of feathers of her who will perch on the
seat underneath which you are, and escape out of the garden;
but mind and take this amulet and tie it to your arm, for the
owner of the dress is Nuzhat-ez-Zeman, my companion at the
philosopher Zirajjan's, who will discover the loss of the dress
as soon as she comes out of the water, and follow you, and
try all her magic arts upon you to destroy you, for the dress
cannot be replaced; and when all her arts fail she will say to
you, 'What want you here?' and you will answer, 'I wish
for some of the apples of this garden;' and she will say,
'Give me the dress then;' and you will say, 'Yes, when I
have the apples.'   Then she will go and return with the
apples, and you will give her this letter."

Having given him these directions, Badr-el-Maha put
provisions and water into the balloon and took leave of him,
and the balloon arose, and sailed with Mehemet through the
air to his destination.

Now be it known that the locality of this garden had
been disclosed by the philosopher Zirajjan to Nuzhat-ez-
Zeman, who, as we have said, was his favourite, and whom
he loved so tenderly for her great proficiency in all the
sciences he had taught her, that he could not find it in
his heart to part with her.   So he gave her a dress of feathers
such as we have described, and a similar one to each of her
associates, so that they could by that means travel whithersoever they wished in one day.   Thus they visited all kinds
of places and countries, but always returned to the philoso-

pher's retreat at night. But the place they most frequented was the " Garden of the Philosophers."

This garden had been planted many ages before by one of the wise men of Greece, who had had a daughter of surpassing beauty, for whom he had sought a place where she might promenade in safety, and had selected this spot, in which he had commanded the genii to make what we have described in it.

They had accordingly brought all kinds of saplings, young plants, and fruits, from all quarters of the earth, and constructed the basin we have mentioned in the centre of the garden. Around this were trees, and statues of metal representing various animals, statues of men in gold and silver, of birds in brass, and land animals in iron; all of them written over with curious names and talismans. The water ran from the mouths of these animals to the basin, describing in its course the most beautiful writing, as if instructed in the art of the pen, and watered in its course the garden, and the shady trees and sweet-smelling flowers to be found there.

No man, however, had ever entered this garden, and had he, he would have surely died, for, so was it ordered, that if any man entered there, he was immediately deprived of the power of motion and destroyed, be he the strongest man in the world. Thus no stranger had ever tasted of the fruit of that garden, and Nuzhat-ez-Zeman and her companions were the only ones who now enjoyed them.

But to return to Mehemet. When he entered the balloon it flew off with him, and sailed through the air until it stopped over the gate of the garden. He immediately alighted and went into the garden, and walked amongst the fruits and flowers, but when he tried to catch them they eluded his grasp. Thus he came to the basin in the centre of the garden, and saw the wondrous statues round it, and the trees, and the seats, as has been described.

Then he went up to the highest of the seats and hid himself under it, and it was of ivory, studded with nails of gold and jewels, and had belonged to the daughter of the Grecian philosopher, who had built the garden for her. The other seats were of wood of aloes, fastened with nails of silver.

And Mehemet looked, and saw that each was overshadowed by a leafy tree, the branches of which were full of singing birds of precious stones, who poured forth musk and amber as they sang. And lo! a flock of ten birds came and perched one on each of the seats, and the largest and most beautiful came and perched on the seat under which Mehemet was.

Then the birds began to sing, and poured forth the musk and amber from their mouths; and the ten birds began to divest themselves of their feathers, and came forth ten beautiful maidens, and went down to the basin to bathe; and she who came forth from the feathers of the largest bird was like unto the full moon in beauty, and more lovely than all, and this was Nuzhat-ez-Zeman.

Then, when they had gone down to the water, and left their dress of feathers behind them on their seats, Mehemet came forth from under the seat and stole the dress of feathers left by Nuzhat-ez-Zeman, and escaped out of the garden, and remained waiting without until they should come forth from the water.

After some time, the damsels came forth out of the water, and began to put on their feathers; but when Nuzhat-ez-Zeman came out she could find her feathers nowhere, although she searched the garden from end to end and all around. At last Mehemet cried out to her, and said, "O beautiful lady! delight of my soul! I have your feathers."

Then Nuzhat-ez-Zeman was greatly incensed, and tried all her magic arts upon him to entrap him. She enticed him by all her blandishments to enter the garden, but in vain— neither her magic nor her charms affected Mehemet.

At last she said, "What want you of me?" Mehemet answered, "I want ten of the apples of the 'Garden;' give me only these, and I will restore your feathers to you."

Then she left him, but his image had in the meantime been graven upon her heart, and she returned and gave him ten of the apples of the garden as he had asked, and said, "Who art thou that thou couldst withstand all my powers of magic, and how learnt you to do this?"

Mehemet answered, "O beautiful lady, I know not myself, but I have a letter with me for you, which, perhaps, may explain the mystery;" and he drew forth the letter from Badr-el-Maha and gave it to her, and the letter was written in a hand known only to the three princesses.

Then she took the letter from Mehemet, and opened it, and it ran as follows :—

"Salutation from Badr-el-Maha to her dear sister Nuzhat-ez-Zeman. Thou mayest remember, O sister, that when we were together—thou, and I, and Durat-el-Muluk—at the philosopher Zirajjan's, we prayed that we might eventually be under the same roof. Now God has heard this prayer, so far as concerns me and Durat-el-Muluk, for we are now under the same roof, wives of the bearer of this letter. We hope that you will complete our happiness and accomplish our destiny by coming also to live with us, for, excepting this, we have naught to wish for. Refuse not, then, the goodness of Providence, but come and live with us; and when you come, we have many things to tell you of what has happened to us, which we cannot tell you now. Peace be with you!"

When Nuzhat-ez-Zeman had read the letter, and understood it, she looked towards Mehemet, and thought what happiness it would be to live with him, for she was attracted by his great beauty; and she said to him, "You come from the princesses Badr-el-Maha and Durat-el-Muluk?"

"Yes, O beautiful lady; what are your commands?" replied Mehemet.

Now all this time Nuzhat-ez-Zeman had been looking at Mehemet, and every moment her love increased towards him, till at last she said, "Enter thy balloon, and I will dismiss these damsels, and follow thee, so that no one may know that I have gone with thee, for I fear if the philosopher Zirajjan learn my intention he will prevent me from coming."

So Mehemet entered the balloon, and pressed the spring as Badr-el-Maha had done, and departed, but his heart was with Nuzhat-ez-Zeman.

But to return to Nuzhat-ez-Zeman. She hid her dress of feathers in some bushes, and returned to the garden and told the young maidens that she had lost it, and that she supposed some large bird had carried it off. "Go now," said she, "and return to the philosopher Zirajjan, and tell him what has happened to me, and that I intend to stay here and go into my observatory to endeavour to make a new one, and that I will return in seven days."

The damsels answered, "To hear is to obey," and departed, leaving her in the garden.

No sooner had they gone than Nuzhat-ez-Zeman put on her

dress of feathers and set out after Mehemet, and soon came up with him.

When Mehemet saw her his heart leapt with joy, and he said to himself, "O Mehemet, God has indeed blessed thee."

Then they continued to sail through the air till they came to the city in which Mehemet's palace was, and they descended just at sunrise, and they were welcomed by Badr-el Maha and Durat-el-Muluk, who had come out to meet them.

Then Mehemet expressed his wish that Nuzhat-ez-Zeman should live with them; and Badr-el-Maha and Durat-el-Muluk both said the pleasure it would give them.

So they assembled the people of the city, and called witnesses, and drew up the contract of marriage, and Mehemet was united to Nuzhat-ez-Zeman that very day.

The next day, which was the tenth of the appointed time, Mehemet said, "I must go and take the apples to the king."

But Nuzhat-ez-Zeman said, "Nay, what need to go so soon; the space is forty days, and I want you to stay with me."

So Mehemet stayed till the forty days were complete, and then took the apples and put them in a dish, and gave them to his slaves to carry, and set out.

During the time of Mehemet's absence, the king had said every day to his vizier Mushir, "I will send and fetch this fellow's wives, for he will never return."

But the vizier Mushir replied, "O most great and gracious monarch, act not rashly, and do nothing until the allotted term be complete."

And while they were thus speaking, behold, Mehemet came and saluted the king, and laid the apples before him.

Then one of the other viziers stepped forward and said, "Are these apples from the 'Garden of the Philosophers?'"

Mehemet replied, "Yes."

This vizier, who was the same who had counselled the king to send Mehemet on this errand, said, "We shall soon see that," and cut a slice off one of the apples, and presented it to the king; and, behold, the apple became whole again, to the astonishment of every one, and the confusion of the vizier.

Mehemet stayed some days, and then took his leave of the king, and returned to his palace and the three princesses.

After he had gone, the king said to his viziers, "Well, what think you now of this fellow; there is no getting rid of him. And, behold, there is nothing he cannot do."

Then the vizier Mushir replied, "O king, thou knowest that I always counselled thee not to attempt the life of this man, for that it was useless, and would bring evil and trouble upon thee eventually, as he is the favourite of Fortune. Now I beg of your majesty, for your own safety, to desist from all further designs against him."

In the meantime the news of Mehemet's return safe and sound from his expedition spread far and wide, and his friends came to congratulate him. Amongst others came the musicians of the king, and Mehemet received them as before with great cordiality, and regaled them sumptuously, as he did all strangers; and they took out their instruments, and struck the chords, and played; and the three princesses came out to hear the music, and the musicians showed their astonishment at seeing another beauty, even more fair than the other two: and Mehemet, heated with the wine he had been drinking, said to them, "You see that the king, by his evil designs and his wish to destroy me, has done me great service; for the first time I brought back a great beauty, and this time I have brought back a greater beauty still, without doing myself the slightest harm."

The next morning Mehemet liberally rewarded the musicians, and dismissed them. On their return they went before the king, who had sent for them to comfort him in his grief, and to dispel his melancholy.

After they had played some time, the king asked them if they had been to Mehemet (for a man always loves to talk about what occupies his thoughts), and they related to him how they had passed the night, and how Mehemet had brought back a third wife, more beautiful even than the two first ; and they expatiated on her beauty till they augmented the chagrin of the king a thousand-fold, and he nearly went mad. He could hide his secret no longer, and sent for his two viziers, and said to them, "I can endure this no longer ; I will have Mehemet executed, happen what may. Whoever opposes me in my design I will kill also."

Then the vizier Mushir saw that the king would not abandon his project of killing Mehemet, and was all the more grieved as he could not oppose him. He knew that the king would bring about his own ruin, for he had the greatest confidence in Mehemet, and was sure that he possessed some divine secret, and that the king would indubitably perish in this attempt on his life.

So he took up the conversation, and said to the king, "As you have determined to kill this man, I will not counsel you not to kill him ; but at least allow me to point out to you the best means of doing so, for to kill a man without any pretext is a grave affair."

Then the king asked Mushir what means he proposed, and the vizier replied, "Send for Mehemet, and say, 'There cannot be two kings in one country. If you wish to remain in this country, I require you to build me a palace formed of alter-nate bricks of silver and gold, which must be situated a mile from here, on the sea-shore, and united to my palace by an arch of a mile in length. Around the arch must be fruit-trees from all parts of the world, bearing all kinds of fruit, even those out of season. If you build this palace, I will be under you; if you do not, you must leave your palace and quit the country.' If he accept the proposal, and promise to build the palace, you will grant him only forty days—a space in which it is humanly impossible to build such a palace. Then put men in ambush along the roads, so that if he attempt to fly before the forty days they may kill him and carry off his wives; but if he remain the forty days, and come and say, 'I am unable to build this palace,' you will let him depart; but as soon as he is gone you can send soldiers after him to kill him and carry off his wives. Thus no one will be able to blame you, and we shall not be exposed to the vengeance of his father. If, however, he build the palace in the forty days, according to your proposal, which I do not believe he can, it will be a fresh proof that if you even were to assemble all your armies you could not hurt him; and in this case it would be better to resist the temptation of the devil, and to take this man as an ally to preserve you against the vicissitudes of fortune."

By this advice the vizier Mushir only wished to bring the affair to an end by exciting Mehemet against the king till he could bear it no longer.

The king thought the vizier's proposal excellent; and in the meantime the vizier Mushir sent a letter secretly to Mehemet, and communicated to him all that had taken place, and how the king had resolved to kill him and carry off his wives.

"If you have the power to build the palace," said he, "remain, and fear nothing; but if you have not, you will certainly perish if you remain. If you wish to fly, let me know, so that I may assist you."

When Mehemet received this letter, he first read it to himself, and then went to the apartment of the princesses and read it to them. The two first princesses remarked "That it was now for Nuzhat-ez-Zeman to act."

She replied that nothing was easier, and that if the king sent for Mehemet on the morrow and made him the proposal, he should say, "That he would do it with great pleasure, that he was ready to do whatever the king ordered." Having given this answer, he must wait for her instructions, and she doubted not all would go well.

The next morning, as Mehemet was sitting in his palace, behold, two pages of the king entered and saluted him, and said, "The king, our master, desires to see you."

Mehemet arose, mounted his horse, and repaired immediately to the royal palace, and having entered the king's presence, saluted him respectfully.

The king received him with great honour, and having retired with him to a cabinet, he said to him, "O King Mehemet, I must tell you frankly that there cannot be two kings in one country, so that if you wish to remain in this country you must build a palace on the sea-coast for me, a mile from here, made of bricks of silver and gold, and join it to this palace by an arch, surrounded by fruit-trees from all parts of the world. If you build this palace, I will be under your rule, but if you cannot, you must leave the country, for we cannot both reign here."

While thus speaking he could not help showing the hostile feelings he bore towards Mehemet.

Then Mehemet answered, "O king of the age, I am ready to obey your orders, but I must beg of your majesty to grant me forty days, after which all shall be ready, and then I will leave you, for I see you have not the same friendly feelings towards me as you had formerly; and thus I hope we shall separate good friends."

So Mehemet took leave of the king, and returned to the three princesses, and recounted to them all that had happened.

The princess Nuzhat-ez-Zeman said, "How can you bear with this miserable traitor? Give me permission to annihilate him, and put you in his place as king of this country."

"If you can do so, do," answered Mehemet; "for otherwise he will undoubtedly kill me at last."

"Wait," answered she, "until I have done what he has asked, and then you will see what I will do."

Then Nuzhat-ez-Zeman turned towards the princesses Durat-el-Muluk and Badr-el-Maha, and said, "I have formed a great plan for this traitor's destruction, which I am now about to put in execution, but you must let me have Mehemet for forty days in order to accomplish it; afterwards the king will be no more, and then Mehemet will reign in his place. Will you grant me this?"

"Yes, yes," replied they, "if it be only for forty days."

Things being thus arranged, Mehemet and the princesses passed the evening in feasting and rejoicing, and when night came retired to rest.

The next morning the princess Nuzhat-ez-Zeman proposed an excursion into the country. Mehemet suggested that it would be better to begin to build the palace without loss of time; but she answered, "Never mind the palace, when it is time I will let you know."

Then they passed the day enjoying themselves. The next morning Nuzhat-ez-Zeman proposed to go hunting, and Mehemet again said to her that she would have plenty of time for hunting when she had finished the palace.

"No, no," replied she; "we have plenty of time for the palace, let us enjoy ourselves now."

Thus they passed thirty-nine days, one day going out to the country, another hunting, another sailing on the sea, and so on, till the eve of the fortieth day.

Mehemet began now to be anxious, and on the evening of the thirty-ninth and last day, he took the princess Nuzhat-ez-Zeman into his cabinet, threw himself at her feet, and said, "I conjure you by the love you bear me, to tell me if you cannot build the palace, so that I may fly and save myself."

"Rise," said she; "be a man. I have ordered a palace to be built in one of my manufactories: when it is ready they will come and let you know. Rest quiet till then, and torment yourself no more. You ought to know, my dear Mehemet, that your life is very precious to me, and that I am incapable of neglecting such a grave affair."

Then Mehemet was comforted by these words.

As for the king, during this time he rose early every morning, and went up on the terrace of the palace to see if there were any signs of the palace; and when on the thirty-ninth day he saw that nothing had yet been done, he was in raptures. "At last," said he, "we have succeeded; I should like to know how he will escape this time, and prevent me from getting his wives."

The last night the princess Nuzhat-ez-Zeman took some powder and scattered it over Mehemet, and threw him into a deep sleep, and then mounted to the top of the palace and rubbed an enchanted ring, which she wore on her finger. Immediately a genius of immense height, who was the slave of the ring, presented himself, and said, " Order, madam, and your orders shall be obeyed."

Then Nuzhat-ez-Zeman said, "I desire you to build a palace of alternate bricks of silver and gold, on the sea-coast, one mile distant from the king's palace, and united to it by an arch, surrounded by fruit-trees from all parts of the world. All this you must do before the day breaks."

" On my head be it," replied the genius, and retired.

Now the genius commanded seventy thousand of the most skilful spirits to assemble, and in the twinkling of an eye they came together. Then he ordered ten thousand to go and fetch all the gold and silver which was in the mines of the earth, and to make it into bricks, ten thousand to dig the foundation of the palace, ten thousand others to lay the bricks of the palace, and ten thousand others those of the arch. Ten thousand he sent to different parts of the world to fetch fruits and flowers, superintending all himself; and before two hours all was complete.

Then he presented himself before the princess Nuzhat-ez-Zeman, and said, " Madam, the palace is ready."

" Very good," replied she; " but there remains still one thing for you to do: I wish you to construct a raft on the sea, capable of containing the king and all the grandees of the empire.   You will then place a table covered with all kinds of viands on it, and connect the raft with the palace by a causeway."

The genius set out at once, and did what she desired.

When day broke she came and woke Mehemet, and presented him with warm water to make his ablutions in.

Poor Mehemet was in great anxiety to know if she had heard from her manufactory, and observed to her that it was the last day, and that he must give an answer to the king.

Then Nuzhat-ez-Zeman took his hand and led him to the top of the palace, and showed him the palace at a distance. The rays of the sun which had just risen were reflected by the bricks of gold and silver, and produced a dazzling effect.

Mehemet at this sight could not believe his own eyes, and began to rub them as if to make sure of what he saw.   He observed to Nuzhat-ez-Zeman that the workmen in her manufactory must be very skilful, and threw himself on her neck and embraced her.

Then Nuzhat-ez-Zeman told Mehemet to mount on horseback and go to the king's palace, and say to him, "O king of the age, the palace which your majesty desired is ready, and I beg of you and the grandees of your empire to come and be my guests on this day."

Mehemet accordingly mounted on horseback, and took the road to the royal palace.

As for the king, a great noise which arose throughout the city from crowds of people flocking from all quarters to admire the palace, awoke him.

And he inquired what was the cause of the noise; and the

vizier Mushir answered, "My liege, the palace which you desired Mehemet to build has arisen this night. We beseech your majesty therefore to give up your passion, and to torment this young man no more, for he who can do such things must needs be resistless." The vizier knew very well, however, that the king Gulnar had but little time to live.

Hardly had they finished speaking when Mehemet entered, saluted the king, and said, "I beg of your majesty to come and see your palace, and to do me the honour of being my guest, you and all the grandees of your empire."

The king accepted the invitation, ordered the grandees to assemble, and repaired to Mehemet's.

Mehemet had warned Mushir not to be of the party, so when the king departed he stayed behind; and when the king asked why he did not come, he replied, "I will follow your majesty." So Mehemet took King Gulnar and his suite into the palace.

The king was so astonished at what he saw that he was almost beside himself; he could not believe his eyes, and could not conceive how that what he saw had all been built in one night.

Mehemet was about to sit down to table when the princess Nuzhat-ez-Zeman told him to retire, and go to the vizier Mushir, who was waiting for him in the city. Then she ordered the genii to remove the planks from beneath their feet, and the king Gulnar and all his grandees were immediately precipitated into the sea—not one escaping.

Half way to the city Mehemet met the vizier Mushir coming at the head of the great men of the city, leading a horse richly caparisoned—destined for Mehemet, who had been proclaimed king.

The vizier Mushir, who foresaw that King Gulnar would return no more, had assembled the great men of the city, his friends, and related to them what had happened, and that the king would return no more; and he suggested to them that it would be well to proclaim Mehemet king; and as soon as it was known that the king Gulnar had been drowned, Mehemet was proclaimed.

Accordingly, when Mushir met Mehemet he told him to mount the horse, and not to punish the innocent for the guilty, so much the more as the people had already declared in his favour.

Then Mehemet was conducted with great pomp to the palace of the government, and mounted the throne, and became king, and made Mushir his prime vizier.

Then he sent and removed the princesses and his furniture to the royal palace; and, as he had great confidence in his vizier Mushir, who was a great statesman, he often left the management of affairs to him, and retired to enjoy the pleasures of domestic life with his family.

Behold what happened to Mehemet, whom we will now leave for a short time.

There were in the city of the late King Gulnar many merchants from the kingdom of King Fidous, who heard the crier proclaiming Mehemet, son of King Fidous, king instead of Gulnar; and, astonished at this, they said to themselves, "How can the son of our king become king instead of Gulnar?" and, when they returned, the first thing they did was to go to the king and give him the glad tidings that his son had been proclaimed king in the place of King Gulnar. King Fidous was greatly surprised, and told them that he had but one son, who was with him.

The merchants replied, "We dare assure your majesty that we have heard the public crier proclaiming your son king in that city."

Then the king sent spies to bring him tidings of what was passing in the city of the late King Gulnar; and, when they returned, they confirmed the report of the merchants, which still more increased the surprise of King Fidous.

"By Allah!" said he, "I will go myself and see who this fellow is who pretends to be my son, and what this all means."

So he mounted on horseback, and, having disguised himself, repaired, at the head of a small troop, to the kingdom of Mehemet; and as on the road every one spoke of Mehemet, son of King Fidous, he at last almost believed it himself, and said, "Perhaps, some time, one of my slaves has been with child, and, fearing her companions, has hidden her condition. However it may be, I will see this pretended son of mine, and speak to him."

Having dressed himself in his royal robes, he sent to tell Mehemet that his father King Fidous had come, and wished to speak to him.

At this news Mehemet was thunderstruck with amazement, and went directly to the apartment of the princesses, and told them what had happened.

"Fear not," said the princess Durat-el-Muluk; "put yourself at the head of the army, and go out and meet him, and receive him with great pomp, as a son should receive his father. In the meantime we will think of what is to be done."

Mehemet, accordingly, with the great men of the city, went forth to receive King Fidous, and, moreover, gave

orders for the happy event to be celebrated by public rejoicings and a general illumination of the town.

The people rejoiced all the more as they knew that there
had been a misunderstanding between Mehemet and his
father, and thought that the father came to be reconciled to
his son.

When Mehemet and Fidous met, they alighted from their
horses, saluted one another, and embraced in the most cordial
manner, like father and son. Then they remounted, and
entered the town with the greatest pomp.

Mehemet conducted his supposed father, King Fidous, to
his palace, and gave him the most beautiful of the apartments
of the palace. Mehemet, during all this time, had addressed
King Fidous as his father.

After supper, Mehemet gave orders to the musicians to
play before his father, and the three princesses danced, and
enchanted King Fidous by their grace and elegance. When
they had finished, Mehemet and King Fidous retired alone,
and King Fidous said to Mehemet, "My dear son—for thou
sayest thou art my child, and I am indeed proud to have
such a son—as I know nothing about thee, I must beg
of thee to tell me how I became thy father, and to hide
nothing, for thy history must be very interesting."

At that moment Durat-el-Muluk entered the cabinet, and,
seeing that Mehemet was at a loss what to say, she took up
the conversation, and related their history from beginning to
end.

Having finished her recital, she said, "Your majesty will
excuse us for having made use of your name. Necessity
compelled us to have recourse to your great reputation, for
without your name we should have infallibly perished. It

is true that we have gained a kingdom by your renown; but, sire, we have no need of this kingdom, and if your majesty wish to reign here, we will be your majesty's most devoted servants. Your majesty sees that we only ask to be left tranquil and happy. We are certain that such a wise and clement king as yourself will be far from disturbing our felicity. Still, your majesty must not think that we are unable to defend ourselves."

Then the princess Nuzhat-ez-Zeman entered the cabinet, and Durat-el-Muluk spoke to her in an unknown tongue, and told her to show her skill.

So she made a sign, and King Fidous thought he was in a great desert, naked, bareheaded, and surrounded by a great number of lions, tigers, and leopards, and he thought he climbed up a tree which stood near, but when he arrived at the top, a bird, as large as a camel, came and took him in its claws, and flew away with him in the air, and having crossed the sea, left him in an island inhabited by ghouls and dives, who, as soon as they saw him, showed their teeth and rushed upon him to devour him. Then he thought that he plunged into the sea and swam for seven days. On the eighth day, when nearly exhausted, he reached an island, naked, bare-footed, and starving, and he found nothing to eat but grass. When night came, a prodigious number of grasshoppers and mosquitos came out, and greatly annoyed him, and to escape from them he mounted a tree and passed the night there.

The next morning he perceived a vessel coming towards the island to take in fresh water, and when it came to the shore he descended from the tree, and begged of the seamen to take him off the island; and they had pity on him, and took him on board, and carried him to their country.

When he arrived in this country, he obtained employment in a bath to light and attend to the fires, and had remained there about twelve months, when one day he saw the body of a dead man lying at the door of the bath. He stopped, to assure himself what it was, and while he was looking at it, the guard coming up, seized him, and brought him before the king, charging him with the death of the man.

He protested his innocence, and swore that he had not committed the murder; but the king, nevertheless, condemned him to death. The executioner having bound his eyes, was just about to give him the fatal blow, when King Fidous made a convulsive start, as if to avoid the blow, and awoke, and saw himself beside Mehemet and the princesses. Then he was greatly amazed and perplexed, and the princess Nuzhat-ez-Zeman asked him what he thought of what he had seen, whether, if she liked to kill him, she could; "for," said she, "it is I who have caused you to see this vision, to let you see my power, and to prevent you from having evil intentions towards us like King Gulnar, who brought his misfortunes on himself."

After this, she again offered him to take the kingdom if he wished, and promised that Mehemet would be his most faithful auxiliary.

Then King Fidous addressed Mehemet, and said, " If thou hadst even been my son, I could not have loved thee better than I do. The possession of the kingdom is not sufficiently tempting to make me lose your friendship for it. On the contrary, I wish to adopt you as my son, and, although a son is generally inferior to the father, I shall always consider you the superior."

"No, no," replied Mehemet; "thou shalt be my superior as a father and a king."

The day when they went to the divan, Mehemet made King Fidous sit in the most exalted place, and sat himself below him, as is the duty of a son to a father.

Now none of the inhabitants of this city discovered the secret, but all thought that the father had come to be reconciled with his son, which gave Mehemet still more consideration in their eyes.

When King Fidous wished to return to his kingdom, Mehemet said to him, "By Allah! I can never more be separated from thee, and I would like much to see your kingdom, and to remain with you; I will, therefore, appoint the vizier Mushir my viceroy, and accompany you."

King Fidous having accepted this proposal with rapture, Mehemet made his preparations, and departed with the princesses, who mounted into their balloon.

As for the two kings, they mounted on horseback and rode.

When they came within a short distance of the capital, the great men of the city and the army came out to meet them, and conducted them to the city with great pomp.

The king gave out that Mehemet was his son by one of his concubines, who had concealed his birth for fear of the jealousy of her companions, and ordered public rejoicings for seven days.

He gave Mehemet a magnificent palace and a post at court as his son. Thus he became the real ruler of the whole of the two kingdoms, and lived in great happiness, surrounded by his family.

*   *   *   *   *   *

But we must now return to the philosopher Zirajjan.

The reader knows that he had loved the princess Nuzhat-ez-Zeman tenderly, and that he had looked upon her as his own daughter.

When she told her companions to return, and say that she had lost her dress of feathers, and that she was going to retire into solitude to make another, they failed not to inform the philosopher, and he believed the tale, and waited seven days for the princess; but when at last he saw that she did not return, his heart was consumed by the fire of grief.

And he said to the damsels, "Go and see what has become of Nuzhat-ez-Zeman, for it is now more than seven days since we have seen her."

The young maidens put on their dresses of feathers and went to the garden, and as they could find no trace of her, returned to the philosopher Zirajjan.

On hearing this he was in the greatest perplexity, and feared lest some other philosopher had carried her off to spite him. Then he consulted his instruments of magic, and found that she had married a man by her own free will. He was just about to mount into his balloon to go in search of her, when he received a letter from the brother of the princess Badr-el-Maha, who, not having been visited by his sister for a long time, was in great anxiety about her, and not knowing where she lived had despatched the following letter to Zirajjan :—

"After the usual compliments, I have to inform you that my sister Badr-el-Maha, since the day of her father's death, has been disgusted with this country, and chosen a retired spot where she built a palace to live in. She was in the habit of coming every month to spend three days with me, but she has not been to see us now for a long time; and as I fear some evil must have happened to her, I beg of you to come to me, in order that we may consult together on the best thing to be done."

When the philosopher received this letter, instead of going in search of Nuzhat-ez-Zeman, he repaired to the brother of Badr-el-Maha, who welcomed him with great cordiality, and told him all the affair.

Then the philosopher consulted his instruments, and found that the princess Durat-el-Muluk had written a letter to the princess Badr-el-Maha, and that she had gone to her. Moreover, he discovered that the three princesses were in the same place, and that they had all married the same man—a distinguished prince; and he thought they must be at the princess Durat-el-Muluk's, in the City of the Four Towers, in the country of King Hassan.

So Zirajjan the philosopher said, " I must go and see them ;" and the brother of Badr-el-Maha having manifested the same desire, they both mounted the balloon, and set out for the City of the Four Towers.

The philosopher Zirajjan went immediately to King Hassan, who received him most graciously.

Then the philosopher asked to see the princess Durat-el-Muluk. " What !" cried the king, " is she not with you?"

" No, no," replied Zirajjan ; " she is not with me, and I have not seen her since the time you sent to fetch her."

Then King Hassan was lost in astonishment, and knew not what to think.

Here we must remark that when Durat-el-Muluk left her father's palace, he missed the two horses the next morning, but, as he found a letter in her room, written in her handwriting, which said that she was going to the philosopher's, her master, he was not troubled about her; but now that he heard from the philosopher that she was not with him, and that he had not seen her for two years, he was greatly .perplexed.

Then the philosopher told him that the brother of Badr-el-Maha had written him a letter, inquiring after his sister, who was missing, like Durat-el-Muluk and the princess Nuzhat-ez-Zeman; and that he, having consulted his instruments, and found that they were all in one spot with Durat-el-Muluk, married to the same husband, thought that they must be there; and he, therefore, had come to inquire about them.

Then King Hassan said, "O philosopher of the age, I be-. seech you to let me hear from them, in whatever place they may be, for I am impatient to know what has become of them."

"I am more impatient than you," answered the philosopher Zirajjan, "to know about Nuzhat-ez-Zeman, who is more dear to me than all the world."

Then the philosopher consulted his instruments to find what country they were in; and, having discovered it, was about to get into his balloon and set off, when King Hassan prayed him to take him with him. The philosopher consented, and they all three, the philosopher, the brother of Badr-el-Maha, and King Hassan, mounted into the balloon, and flew off into the air.

The philosopher guided the balloon so skilfully that in a very short time it stopped on the top of the house in which the three princesses were. They arrived towards evening. Then the philosopher left them on the top of the house, and entered alone, and surprised the three princesses in the saloon, who, as soon as they saw him, arose and saluted him, and kissed his hands respectfully.

Then said he to them, "What have you done?"—"We have but done the will of God," replied they. "It was our fate, and we beg of you to sit down, that we may tell you all that has happened, for our history is truly extraordinary, and fit to serve as an example to posterity."

"I cannot sit down," replied he to Durat-el-Muluk, "for your father and the brother of Badr-el-Maha are waiting for me on the top of the house."

"Then," said they, "we beg of you to manage this affair for us."

So the philosopher went out, and ascended to the top of the house, and brought back his companions with him to the saloon.

When the two princesses saw their relations, Durat-el-Muluk kissed her father's hand, and was ashamed, and Badr-el-Maha saluted her brother.

Then King Hassan asked his daughter why she had acted thus, and the brother of Badr-el-Maha put the same question to his sister.

And the princess Durat-el-Muluk spoke, and said, "I will relate our history, which is truly an extraordinary one, for I have been the chief actor in this affair." So she related to her father, and all those who were present, that as he had forbidden her to marry her cousin, whom she loved, she had formed the project of flying with him, and how they had given one another rendezvous in the garden, and by what chance she had taken Mehemet for her cousin, how they had not spoken the whole night on account of the rain, how she had made the discovery the next morning that he was not her cousin when it was too late to return, and that when she found him to be an upright and noble man she had been legally married to him; in short, she recounted the whole affair from beginning to end.

When she had finished, Badr-el-Maha related to her brother her history, how she had received the message from Durat-el-Muluk, and accompanied Mehemet to discover the enchanted sabre, how he had killed the giant, and how she had married Mehemet to live with Durat-el-Muluk; in short, she related her history from beginning to end.

When she had finished, Nuzhat-ez-Zeman narrated to the philosopher Zirajjan her story, and the others listened; she told him how Mehemet had hidden himself under the chair, how she had given him the apples, and that if she had married him it was only to be with her two companions, Durat-el-Muluk and Badr-el-Maha; thus she brought their history up to that time.

This marvellous tale greatly surprised the philosopher Zirajjan, King Hassan, and the brother of Badr-el-Maha.

All this took place unknown to Mehemet and his adopted father during their absence.

When he arrived at the palace, Badr-el-Maha went to meet him, and informed him that the father of Durat-el-Muluk and her brother, and the philosopher Zirajjan, had come, and were in the saloon of the palace, and told him to enter and receive them.

So he entered and saluted them, and they arose and saluted him, and they saw at once that he was a king by his noble appearance and distinguished manners, which captivated them completely.

The philosopher Zirajjan observed to the company that the

best thing a girl could have was a good husband, and that the
three princesses had only obeyed their destiny; in which they
all acquiesced.

As King Hassan, the brother of Badr-el-Maha, and the
philosopher liked Mehemet, they stayed with him three
days—three of the most happy they had ever passed in
their lives.

When it was time for them to depart, the philosopher
Zirajjan said that he also would like to be near Nuzhat-ez
Zeman, from whom he could not separate. The brother of
Badr-el-Maha and King Hassan expressed also their desire to
do the same, but as the princesses said they could not be
separated from one another, they deliberated as to what they
should do.

Then the philosopher Zirajjan spoke, and said, "There is
but one way to satisfy all, which is, for the three princesses,
with their husband, to go and live in the City of the Towers
with King Hassan, and for us all to go and live there also.
This proposal was unanimously agreed to, and they accordingly
began to make their preparations for the journey.

Mehemet went to his adopted father and informed him of
the arrival of his relations, and King Fidous invited them to
his palace and welcomed them cordially, and regaled them for
many days.

When he learnt that they had determined on going, he
said that he would not oppose it, although separation from
his adopted son would cause him great grief.

Mehemet said that it gave him also great pain to part from
his adopted father, but he could not displease Durat-el-Muluk,
to whom he owed so much.

King Fidous replied, "Do what you will, my son, for the

kingdom is your kingdom, and the country is your country, and no one shall be my successor but you."

So they all took leave of King Fidous, and mounted into the balloon and departed.

On the road they called on the vizier Mushir, whom Mehemet recommended to be just in his government, and told to send the revenue to the City of the Towers.

Then they left the vizier Mushir, and arrived at the City of the Towers, and went and lived in the palace of King Hassan, who gave great feasts in honour of their arrival.

He afterwards gave them a magnificent palace to themselves, and the philosopher Zirajjan took up his abode in the city to be near Nuzhat-ez-Zeman. He ordered the genii to build him a great palace in a beautiful spot, and to divide it into three suites of apartments, one for each of the princesses.

Mehemet was always given the title of King Mehemet, and had a great train of attendants and followers.

The philosopher sent to his country, and transported to the City of the Towers all his property and his disciples.

The brother of Badr-el-Maha also went to his country, and appointed his vizier his viceroy, and ordered him to send him the revenue every year to the City of the Towers, where he had taken up his abode.

When they were thus settled, King Hassan sent for the philosopher Zirajjan, and said to him, "You know, my dear Zirajjan, that I am advanced in years, and that I have no children but Durat-el-Muluk, whom Mehemet has married, and thus become my son-in-law; behold, now, I wish to abdicate in his favour."

The philosopher replied, "Do what you think right, O king."

G

Then the king assembled all the great men of his kingdom, and the army, and told them that, as he was advanced in years, and wished to devote his time to religion, he had adopted his son-in-law as his son, and appointed him his successor, abdicating in his favour.

The great men of the kingdom greatly rejoiced at this news, and congratulated the new king. Mehemet, on his accession to the throne, appointed the brother of Badr-el-Maha his vizier, and ruled with the greatest justice ; and the people had not been so happy for many years as under his government.

One day, however, the inhabitants of the country came rushing to take refuge in the city, saying that a great army of Chinese fire-worshippers, under the command of a king called Abd-en-Nar, were coming towards the city, laying everything waste before them with fire and sword.

This sudden attack was made at the instigation of the cousin of Durat-el-Muluk, whom the reader knows she had given rendezvous to in the garden, and who did not come on account of the rain.

Now, the next morning, having heard that his cousin had disappeared, he guessed that she must have left the town without seeing him, and had not thought proper to return.

So he remained three days in the city to make his uncle think he had nothing to do with her flight, and then went and sought her throughout the dominions of King Hassan, and at last, not having obtained the least information, retraced his steps and returned.

His life, from the night on which she had left the city till she returned with her husband, had been a continual torment to him.

When he learnt that she was married to Mehemet, he became a prey to the bitterest jealousy; but what was his indignation when he heard that King Hassan had abdicated in his favour.

He mounted his horse, left the country, and took the road to Upper China, went and presented himself to King Abd-en-Nar, threw himself at his feet, and asked his protection, relating his history, how his uncle had married his daughter to an unknown foreigner to annoy him, and how he had abdicated in his favour. He added that the kingdom had belonged to his ancestors, and that he was the rightful heir to the crown, that he whom his uncle had adopted was unfit to reign, and concluded by describing the beauty of the country, and by praying Abd-en-Nar to take it and to make him his vassal.

In short, he besought the king with such warmth, that Abd-en-Nar put himself at the head of a great army, invaded the country, and was pushing forward to the City of the Towers.

This was the reason of the country people taking refuge in the city.

As soon as Mehemet heard the news, he consulted with the philosopher Zirajjan as to what was to be done.

The philosopher said, "Let them come and be our prey; but in the meantime we must fortify the town."

So King Mehemet gave orders for the town to be fortified, and prepared himself for the combat.

After a few days a great cloud of dust was perceived, then helmets and spears were seen glistening in the sun, and lastly, a great army, which was advancing on the town.

As soon as these came within shot of the town the inhabitants fired on them, and obliged them to retreat and to take up their position a short distance from the city.

After they had been encamped before the town three days, King Abd-en-Nar sent a herald with a letter to King Hassan, who came to the gate of the city, crying " I am a herald, the bearer of a letter for King Hassan."

The porters went and informed King Mehemet, and he ordered them to admit the herald and conduct him into his presence.

When the herald entered, he gave the letter to Mehemet, who opened it, and found it ran as follows :—

" Praise be to fire and light.

" We, King Abd-en-Nar, command King Hassan to seize the man to whom he has married his daughter, and in whose favour he abdicated, and to send him to us, and to give his daughter and his kingdom to his nephew, and to send the revenue of the kingdom as a tribute to us.

" If you refuse to obey these our commands, we will lay your kingdom waste, and exterminate your race."

As soon as Mehemet had read this letter, he gave it to his father-in-law King Hassan, and to the philosopher Zirajjan, to read. They told him to send a similar letter, for God would surely deliver Abd-en-Nar into his hands.

So Mehemet wrote an answer, gave it to the herald, and dismissed him.

Then he marshalled his troops and made a sortie from the town, his trumpets sounding and drums beating.

He was at the head of the army, and encouraged his troops, who fought like lions.

On his part, the king Abd-en-Nar did the same, and thus the two armies, crying out madly, rushed on one another.

Then the princess Nuzhat-ez-Zeman rubbed her ring, and the genius having come before her and asked what she desired, she ordered him to take a hundred genius, disguised as horsemen, and to attack Abd-en-Nar, and cut his head off, and put it on a spear.

The genius replied, " On my head and my eye be it,'' and withdrew.

When the battle began, the genii attacked Abd-en-Nar, cut his head off, put it on a lance, and began to cry, " O worshippers of fire, behold your king is slain; you have only one means of escaping death—fly!"

When the fire-worshippers heard these words, and saw the head of their king, they lost courage, and, seized with horror, threw down their arms, and gave themselves up prisoners.

The genii also killed the cousin of Durat-el-Muluk, and made great carnage amongst the enemy, and all who were not killed were made prisoners.

Great was the spoil Mehemet took : horses, arms, tents, and provisions, all fell into his hands.

Then he made a triumphant entry into the city, and ordered a public thanksgiving. But the philosopher Zirajjan said to Mehemet, " As we have killed one of the kings of China, we shall never be sure of not being attacked by some of them, so we must take measures to prevent them from harming us, and I have formed a plan for that purpose."

King Mehemet replied, "Do what you please, and may God bless your exertions."

So the philosopher Zirajjan went up into his observatory, and remained there retired for thirty days; then he came out, mounted into the balloon, took his genii with him, and departed for China.

Some time after he returned, with all the princes of China in chains, and presented them to King Mehemet, who asked them one by one what religion they were. If they said they were Mussulmans, he allowed them to return to their country, recommending them to be just, and requiring them to send a yearly tribute; but if they said they were idolaters, he offered them to embrace Islamism, and if they did so, he sent them to their country on the same conditions as the first; but if they refused to become Mussulmans, he had them killed, and put Mussulman princes in their stead.

Thus all Upper and Lower China were annexed to his empire; and he governed with the greatest equity, and became the greatest monarch on the earth.

He lived happily, and strove to make others happy.

Some years after the above events, he received a letter from King Fidous, which ran thus :—

"Salutation from King Fidous to his well-beloved son King Mehemet.

"I have to inform you, my dear son, that I am seriously ill, and that I wish to see you before dying."

King Mehemet showed the letter to King Hassan, his father-in-law, and to the philosopher Zirajjan, who both were of opinion that it was their duty to repair immediately to King Fidous.

The philosopher Zirajjan mounted into his balloon, took King Mehemet and King Hassan with him, and departed for the city of King Fidous, whom they found on his death-bed.

For ten days the philosopher, who was a skilful physician, tried every means to save him; but, as his time was come, all his efforts were ineffectual, and King Fidous expired.

They rendered him the last duties, interred him with great

pomp, and proclaimed his son in his stead; and having confirmed him in his government, left him, and returned to their
country.

Two years after King Hassan fell ill, and when he died he
left his kingdom and all his treasures, his arsenals, his fleets,
and all that he possessed, to his adopted son-in-law Mehemet,
who mourned for his death sincerely, and rendered him the
last duties, and interred him with great pomp in the grave of
his fathers.

Then Mehemet became the monarch of the whole of the
country, but as the grief for the death of his father had not
yet subsided, he resolved to take a journey to alleviate his
sorrow.

So he bethought him of the Kurd tribe amongst whom he
had spent his youth, and of the old man with whom he had
served as a shepherd, and who had given him the five sheep,
and he felt a great desire to see him and reward him; but as
he did not know whether they now dwelt in the same place
or had removed, or were living or dead, he had recourse to
the philosopher Zirajjan, to whom he related all his history,
expressing his desire to him to revisit the country where he
had passed his youth.

The philosopher proposed to him to go with him in his
balloon, and that they should descend whenever they saw a
tribe of Kurds until they found his tribe.

King Mehemet and the philosopher accordingly mounted
into the balloon and departed, after having appointed a
viceroy to reign during the king's absence.

The philosopher had charged the genii to provide them
with provisions and every necessary for the journey.

Thus whenever they saw a tribe of Kurds they descended

a certain distance from them, and then with a hundred genii
in the form of horsemen they approached and demanded to
see the camp, saying that their king was returning from the
chase and wished to visit them.

Then the great men of the tribe used to come and meet
Mehemet and make great feasting in his honour.

In this way Mehemet had the opportunity of seeing all the
tribes, and never failed to give them proofs of his munifi-
cence before he left them.

He then went for a certain distance, dismissed the hundred
genii horsemen, and mounted his balloon with the philosopher Zirajjan to go in search of another tribe.

Thus he saw many tribes, until at last he met the tribe
amongst whom he had been brought up, and whom he had
left six years before.

As soon as he drew nigh to the camp, Mehemet at once
knew the property which he had inherited from his father,
and which he had sold.

The greater part of the tents, horses, and camels, were still
marked with the name of his father Ker Khan.

Now it is natural for a man to love his country and
remember it with pleasure, should he even have left it in
poverty and have returned a king, and this because he has
passed his childhood there.

So Mehemet, when he saw the Kurds, his old companions,
and the goods which once belonged to his father, was touched,
and the tears came into his eyes.

Then the philosopher Zirajjan knew that he had found his
country, and said to him, "Why dost thou weep, for this is
not the millionth part of what thou possessest now?"

King Mehemet replied, "God forbid that I should weep

for goods and chattels; I weep because I think of my father
and mother, and of the days of my childhood; and I cannot
restrain my tears, for youth passes as a dream, and man
knows not its value till it is passed. I swear to you, O philosopher of the age, that all the riches which I possess are
not worth a single day of my youth in my eyes."

"You are right," replied the philosopher; "it is a fact
acknowledged by all people of intellect." .

Hardly had they finished thus conversing when the chief
of the tribe, at the head of his people, came out to meet
them, and took them into a magnificent tent, where a table
was spread with every luxury for their reception.

While they were at table eating and drinking, King Mehemet perceived the old man with whom he had served as a
shepherd, and who had given him the five sheep.

So when they were about to rise from the table, Mehemet
motioned to them to remain, and began to speak to them in
their own language, asking them of what country they were,
and what was their origin.

When they saw that he spoke their language, they had
more confidence in him, and thought that kings must speak
all the languages of the world. Then they spoke to him
frankly, and told him they were from the country around
Aleppo, and that they had been in China for many years.
Now Mehemet had heard this from his father, and asked
them what was the name of the chief under whom they had
come; and they replied, "Ker Khan."

"Did he leave any children?" asked Mehemet. Then the
old man with whom he had served shed tears, and said to
him, "O king of the age, Ker Khan left an only child, called
Mehemet; but, unfortunately, as he was young and inex-

perienced, he wasted the goods which his father left him, and fell into the depth of poverty, and left the country, and I know not what has become of him. If he had only remained, I would have considered him as my son, and I would have helped him in any way." Here the old man melted again into tears, for he loved Mehemet and his father greatly.

At this sight Mehemet could not restrain his tears either, and arose and threw himself on the old man's neck, and cried, "I am Mehemet, son of Ker Khan;" and all the Kurds arose, and were greatly astonished.

Then Mehemet related his history to them, and reproached those who had abandoned him after he had lost his riches, and made them presents, and dismissed them.

Then he turned to the old man, and said, "I always considered you as my father, and now I wish to take you with me, and give you a position at my court. He also offered the tribe to come and live in his city, but they replied, "You know that we cannot inhabit cities, as we are accustomed to live only in the open air; nevertheless, we will come and encamp in your country, and live under your protection."

"You will be welcome," replied Mehemet. The next morning they struck their tents, put them on the camels, and departed; but as they did not know the road, the philosopher Zirajjan bade the genii horsemen accompany them as guides.

The philosopher Zirajjan and Mehemet took the old man, and got into the balloon, and travelled from country to country until they came to the spot where Mehemet had bought the dream; and as the sight of that spot brought back agreeable recollections, he proposed to the philosopher to pass the night there. So they descended, and the genii erected tents and spread a table, and waited on them.

Then Mehemet said to the philosopher, "This is the spot where I bought the dream of a man who was coming—like that one now coming towards us;" and Mehemet pointed to a man who had just appeared coming towards them. What was his surprise to see, when he came nearer, that it was the same who had sold him the dream. However, although he knew him at once, he said nothing.

Now the man, when he had got the five sheep from Mehemet, went and sold them in the next village, and spent the money, and returned to his country. His trade being that of a courier, he was now carrying a packet of dispatches, and, his provisions being out, he approached Mehemet's tent, and sat down until he should be invited to eat.

Mehemet ordered food to be carried to him, and then called him into his tent, and asked him who he was.

"I am a carrier of letters," replied the man. "Very good," said Mehemet. "Will you remain here to-night, and continue your journey to-morrow?"

The man accepted this proposal all the more readily as he was fatigued, and saw that all was comfortable around him.

"You must have travelled a great deal about here," said Mehemet.

"I have done nothing but go and come in this neighbourhood for many years," said the man; "and a strange adventure I once had just near this spot has just come to my recollection. One day, as I was passing this spot, I met a young Kurd, the greatest simpleton, I think, I ever met in the world. He had five sheep with him, and cried out and asked me, as I passed, whence I came and whither I was going. I laughed to myself at his simplicity, and answered that I came from a country, and was going to my destination to catch a dream. At this, thinking a dream was something to be bought and sold, he offered to buy the dream for the five sheep he had with him, which he afterwards gave me to go and catch the dream, and I know not what has become of him from that day since; but I can assure you he was the greatest simpleton that was ever created.

When King Mehemet heard these words, he asked him if he were not frightened of meeting the young Kurd again, who, in that case, would no doubt say that he had not caught the dream, nor found where it was, and demand the five sheep back, or that he should go with him and show him where it was to be found. " What would you do in such a case?" asked Mehemet.

" Oh, it would be very easy to deal with such a fool as he. I would play him another trick, and perhaps would this time strip him of his very clothes, and send him away naked to seek the dream."

On this Mehemet burst out laughing. " Do you know who bought the dream of you?" asked he.

"No, by Allah!" replied the courier.

"It was I," said Mehemet, "who bought the dream of you, and that dream has made my fortune: may God reward you." And thereupon he related his history from beginning to end.

The courier arose, kissed the ground before Mehemet, and said, "It is you have made my fortune, as you can neither forget me nor the adventure of the dream."

" No, indeed," replied Mehemet, "I will not forget you.

But now tell me at last whence come you, and whither go you?"

Then the courier smiled, and said, "I am going to deliver letters in the next town, and to bring the answers, as is my trade."

Mehemet told the philosopher to charge one of the genii to deliver the letters and bring the answers back, which was no sooner said than done, for one of the genii disguised himself as a messenger and executed the commission.

Then Mehemet said to the man, "I wish to make you my courier, and you must come and live with me."

The man replied, "I ask for nothing better; but I have my family."

"Very good; I will send for your family. Now take these letters and distribute them, and afterwards go with these two persons," said Mehemet, pointing to the two genii, "who will bring your family."

The man was transported with joy at this offer, and departed at once with the two genii, went and distributed the letters, and then the two genii transported his family to the city of Mehemet.

Then they all set out for the City of the Towers, and the courier was so rejoiced, that he did nothing but dance and sing all the journey, as if drunk with gladness.

When they came to the city, the whole town came out, and there were feasting and public rejoicings and illuminations for the space of forty days.

Then Mehemet gave a house to the courier for himself and his family, and made him chief of the couriers; and he gave an exalted post at his court to the old man with whom he had lived as a shepherd.

Some time after this, the tribe of the Kurds came with all their flocks, and Mehemet gave them a large district near the town for them to dwell in.

Now as Allah wished to complete the happiness of Mehemet, he granted him three male children, one by Durat-el-Muluk, one by Badr-el-Maha, and one by Nuzhat-ez-Zeman.

This happy event was celebrated throughout the empire by public rejoicings, and when the children grew up, King Mehemet entrusted their education to the philosopher Zirajjan, who spared no pains to perfect them in every science.

Thus was the happiness of Mehemet completed, and the young man who had gone three days without eating or drinking, and who was so simple as to buy a dream for five sheep, came at last to have three of the most beautiful and accomplished princesses for his wives, and reigned over the greatest empire in the world.

May God grant that our readers be as happy as Mehemet, and send them PEACE.

THE PRINCESS AND THE COBBLER.

A TURKISH TALE.

I T was near the close of a summer's day; the last rays of
the setting sun fell like a flood of liquid gold over the
town of Ghazni, gilding its domes and minarets. A cool
refreshing breeze, loaded with the incense of the flowers of
the surrounding country, had sprung up to refresh the weary
groups of porters and water-carriers reposing, after their day's
toil, near the public fountain. The call of the *muezzins* from
the minarets, to assemble the faithful to prayer, had ceased;
and so great was the calm, the quiet which reigned, that one
might have supposed it some enchanted city, o'er which the
magician's rod had waved and brought a spell of slumber
on the whole.

At the door of one of the shops of the main street sat a
young man, cross-legged, as is the custom in the East, smoking his *chibook*, awaiting customers. His noble mien and
majesty of countenance contrasted strangely with his humble
station; for "Said" was a shoemaker, whom, strange to say,
they had thus called, as if in mockery, "The Fortunate."

The fine contour and chiselled features of his countenance,

and the grace of his person, spoke more for his noble descent than would many a patent of nobility, spite of the contradictory evidence of his present condition; for, by the sudden and violent revolution in the East, it not unfrequently happens that the peasant is as well descended as the peer.

Said, also, had the advantages of education, for his father had early sent him to the school of Ghazni, where he had learned to read and write—no slight accomplishment in the East.

On the evening, then, of which we are speaking, Said was about at last to close his shop, when he caught sight of a wandering dervish coming down the street towards his shop. The dervish approached, and, interested by his benevolent face, Said addressed him, and offered to mend a hole which he saw in the dervish's boot.

"Thanks, my son," said the dervish; "God has given thee a good heart, and, in return for your kindness, I will tell thee how to mend a rent in thy heart."

Said invited the stranger to enter, and laid supper before him, and they stayed conversing till near midnight. At last the dervish said, "Behold, thou art called Said, but thy heart is sad, and thou art not satisfied with thy humble fortune; listen, now, and I will tell thee how to mend it. You have read the 'Jihan Numa' and the 'Ajaib Macklukat,'* and you have longed to witness with your own eyes the wonders of foreign lands. Arise, now; to-morrow, sell thy furniture, and set out and see the world; but I counsel you, firstly, choose some trusty companions, for the Prophet has said, 'First the companion, then the road;' secondly, not to

---

* Two well-known geographical books in the East.

sleep in any place where water is not near; and thirdly, not to enter any city towards evening."

The next morning the dervish departed, and Said, having sold his furniture and made his preparations for the road, agreed to set out in company with a party of merchants about to leave the town.

They travelled for a considerable time without meeting with any adventure, when one evening they came to a city, and the merchants hastened to enter before the gates should be closed. Some short distance from the city Said remembered the words of the dervish, not to enter any city at the close of day, and expressed his intention of remaining behind, and not entering the city till the next morning. At first his companions endeavoured to dissuade him from his apparently absurd intention; but at last, finding all their efforts useless, they left him sitting on the bank of a stream, and hastened to the town. The night soon fell black and dreary, and Said found himself alone with his thoughts, for not even the faintest ray of a star enlivened the scene. He arose, and, leaving the bank of the stream, approached the city. Not knowing whither he went, he came at last to the burial-place of the town, and entered, and wandered amongst the tombs for some time.

He had not been there long before the storm, which had been threatening for some hours, burst forth in all its fury. Terrific claps of thunder seemed to rend the very heavens, and flashes of forked lightning illumined the tombs, giving them a grotesque and sinister appearance. To take shelter from the storm, Said descended into one of the sepulchres, somewhat regretting now that he had followed the dervish's advice. At last, unable to control his impatience, he quitted the tomb and came into the open air. Scarcely had he ascended, when he was amazed to see two men letting something down from the wall of the city, which joined the burial-place. He retreated behind the tomb to escape observation, and saw the two men descend, and, taking up their burthen, carry it to the very tomb he had just left. After a short time the two men reappeared, and, passing so close as almost to touch Said, left the burial-place.

Said re-entered the tomb, and, having struck a light, saw that the load which the two men had deposited was a coffin, which lay overturned. The outside of the coffin was stained with blood, and blood seemed to be oozing from beneath it. Said stood some time transfixed with horror; his limbs seemed about to fail him, and he turned so pale that he might himself have been taken for some wandering inhabitant of the tomb. What was his horror when the coffin seemed to move! He approached it, however, and, urged by curiosity, overcame his fears, and turned it upwards, removed the lid, and beheld a beautiful maiden lying in her winding-sheet, the whiteness of which contrasted strongly with the stains of blood and gore upon it. Said had no doubt that the maiden was dead, and began to remove the winding-sheet, when, to his amazement, he thought he heard a faint whisper from the dead body, saying, "Do you not fear God, that you thus uncover me?"

Certain now that it was a living body, Said answered, " O beautiful maiden, art thou in pain? My heart is grieved to see thee in such a condition, and I thought thee dead."

"Canst thou help me?" cried the maiden; "because, if so, do it, and I will be obliged to thee. I am bleeding to death."

Said immediately took off his kaftan, or loose upper garment, and, tearing it in pieces, bound up the wounds of the maiden.

The next morning, at daybreak, Said arose, and, taking up the maiden, entered the city before there was scarcely anyone astir, reached a karavanserai, or Eastern hotel, and deposited his burthen in a room there, telling the keeper that she was his sister, and that they had been attacked by robbers on the road.

In a short time the maiden recovered from her wounds; and one day, returning from the bath, whither she had been for the first time, asked Said to bring pen, ink, and paper, and wrote a note, which she gave him, telling him to go to the exchange, where he would see a certain merchant sitting, whose appearance she described, to whom he should give the note. "Whatever he give you," said she, "take it, and bring it to me."

When Said came to the exchange, sure enough he saw a merchant sitting just in the place the maiden had said, whose appearance corresponded exactly with the description given by her of the person to whom he was to give the note.

Said accosted the merchant, saluted him, and presented the note.

The merchant took the note, kissed it, and put it to his head, as is the custom in the East; and, having perused it, drew forth a purse from his girdle, and gave it to Said.

Said took the purse, as the maiden had directed, and returned to the karavanserai.

"Go now," said the maiden, "and buy a small house, and with what remains of the money purchase clothes for yourself and me."

Said lost no time in complying with her request, and soon the house and clothes were ready, and they removed thither.

Shortly after they had settled in their new abode, the maiden again sat down to write, and, giving a letter to Said, told him to go again, and give it into the hand of the young merchant.

Said went, as before, and gave the letter to the merchant, who took it, and drew forth this time two purses and handed them to Said.

Said returned to the maiden, who said, "Go now and buy horses, clothes, and slaves, and bring them hither."

Said did as she directed, and, when all was completed, the maiden wrote another note, and gave it to Said, who went to the merchant, as before, and returned with three purses of gold.

"Now," said the maiden, "take one of these purses, and go to such a street, where you will find another merchant ; ask to see his wares, and whatever price he demand, give it him."

The young man went and did so, although quite unable to imagine what all this meant.

After a few days, the maiden gave him another of the purses of gold, and told him to go and purchase certain stuffs of the merchant, but not to hesitate, whatever price he might ask.

Said went to the merchant, demanded to see certain stuffs, and, having been shown several descriptions, purchased the most expensive, without attempting to make the merchant abate one farthing of the enormous price he asked, and paid down the money at once.

The merchant, delighted with such a customer, invited Said to come and spend the next evening with him.

Said returned to the maiden, and related what had passed.

"Go," said the maiden; "but take care only to look straight before you, and not on either side."

The next evening Said repaired to the merchant's house, was sumptuously regaled by the merchant, and spent a most pleasant evening, carefully avoiding, however, as the maiden had counselled him, to look about him.

When he returned, he related all that had happened to the maiden, who said, "To-morrow, go and invite him to come here."

Accordingly, when the morrow came, Said repaired to the merchant's, and invited him to spend the evening with him. The merchant replied by saying, "*Bism illah* (in the name of God), I will come."

The young man returned home, and informed the maiden. She immediately set about putting the house in order, prepared wine, fruits, and roast meats, and ordered music to be in readiness.

When evening came, the merchant failed not to keep his appointment, and he and Said remained eating and drinking till near midnight.

At last the merchant arose, and wished to take leave, but Said, whom the maiden had told not to let the merchant depart, pressed him to stay, and on his insisting to go, told him that he should not leave the house that night, but must sleep there; at the same time he ordered cushions to be spread out, and lay down.

The merchant having no other resource, was obliged to yield, and lay down beside him.

In the middle of the night, when the merchant was sleeping soundly, the maiden entered the chamber. Awakened by the rustle of her garments as she passed, Said sat up and watched her. She drew nigh the merchant, and, leaning over him, drew forth a dagger and plunged it into his heart. With one faint groan the merchant expired, without uttering one word or cry.

The maiden turned, and seeing Said sitting up and awake, said to him, "Behold, now, it is time that I tell thee my history, for my doings must, indeed, seem strange to thee. Listen, now, O youth, and judge not before thou hast heard my tale.

" I am the daughter of the king of this city, the last of a long race of mighty sovereigns who have ruled this kingdom. The villain whom thou hast just seen me slay, is the son of a butcher in this city.

" One day, in an evil hour, as I went to the bath, I was attracted by his handsome appearance, which was as fair as his heart was black and wicked, and fell in love with him. It was not long before he discovered the passion I bore for him, and letters passed between us ; and at last he visited me disguised as a girl, and not unfrequently I visited him in disguise. I furnished him with money to establish himself as a merchant, and he became, as you have seen, one of the richest in the city.

" One day I unexpectedly visited him, and, entering his apartment as usual without any announcement, what was my horror, my indignation, after all I had done for him, to see him sitting with another woman, with whom he was so engaged, that it was not until I had been some minutes in the room that he was aware of my presence. I upbraided him with his ingratitude and inconstancy, and struck the woman with whom he was sitting. He said not a word, but left the apartment, returning with two men, who immediately seized me, and, wounding me in several places, placed me in a coffin, believing me dead, and carried me out of the city, over the wall, to the cemetery, and placed me in the tomb, when God sent thee to rescue me. Arise, now; go to my father, and bring him the glad tidings of my discovery: he will not fail to reward thee richly."

On the morning after the princess had gone to her faithless lover, the king missed his daughter, and caused search to be made for her throughout the city and the neighbourhood in vain. Knowing that she must have voluntarily quitted the palace, the king made a vow, that if ever he found her he would marry her to a cobbler to punish her.

When Said came to the palace, he demanded audience of the grand vizier, and imparted to him what he had to tell the king concerning his daughter.

The vizier brought him before the king, who was rejoiced to hear of his daughter's safety, and sent to fetch her immediately. Having satisfied himself of her innocence, he kissed her on both eyes, and welcomed her back to the palace, and repented of the rash vow he had made to marry her to a cobbler to humble her.

After the first burst of joy, the king sat sad and as if embarrassed what to do.

The vizier inquired the cause of his grief, and on his explaining it, told him to rejoice, for it seemed that God had willed that his daughter should be married to Said, as he had been a cobbler in his native town of Ghazni.

Then the joy of the king knew no bounds, and he gave his

daughter to Said, with a large dowry, and made him governor over a large province of his empire.

Thus Said became a king's son, and was rewarded for his goodness to the dervish, and for following his advice.

THE DISPUTED MAIDEN.

IT is related in the old chronicles that four persons—a carpenter, a goldsmith, a tailor, and a hermit—agreed to travel. They accordingly set out, and travelled for some time without any accident happening, till one night they had to sleep in a spot in a mountainous country, the terrific grandeur of whose scenery inspired the beholder with fear.

For fear of the wild beasts, which infested the neighbourhood, they agreed to watch by turns; and, it being the carpenter's turn to watch first, he arose, and took his place as sentinel while the others slept. To dispel the drowsiness which was beginning to steal over him, he took his tools and began carving a figure out of one of the trees which were near, and, giving it a head, feet, and hands, at last produced the image of a young girl.

The time had now come for the goldsmith to watch; and he also, being frightened of falling asleep, began to rub his eyes and look about him, and, whilst so doing, the figure of the girl which his friend the carpenter had cut out of the tree caught his eye. He greatly admired the skill of the car-

penter, and, to prevent his falling asleep, began in his turn
to show his skill in his art, and adorned the figure with ear-
rings, bracelets, and all the ornaments which ladies wear.

By this time the tailor's turn had come to mount guard;
and when he arose, the first thing he saw was the figure of
the girl. Greatly amazed at this sight, he at last said, "I
must not be behind these fellows. I'll let them see what I
can do." So he set to work and made garments of rich ma-
terials befitting the figure, and dressed her in them; and so
natural did she look when he had finished that he did not
recognize her, and almost took her for a thing of life; and
thou also, O reader, if thou hadst been there, wouldst have
thought so, for nothing could have looked more natural.

The time of his watch being now complete, he woke the
hermit, and laid himself down to sleep.

As soon as the hermit opened his eyes he saw the figure,
and, drawing near to look at it more closely, cried in his
admiration, "What see I? A figure to deceive the wise; a
strange image such as I have never seen, the altar of whose
eyebrows would be the *kiblah** of lovers, and the red wine
of whose lips would be food for body and soul."

Then the hermit raised his head towards the court of the
Creator of souls, and prayed, saying, "O Almighty God, possessor of all power and glory, Thou art He who hast brought
man from the void of non-existence to the plain of existence;
Thou art He who hast made fruit to come forth from the dry
trees,—I pray Thee, all great and gracious God, not to let
me be disgraced amongst my companions, and to give unto
this body a soul, and a tongue to sing thy praises."

---

* The *kiblah* is the point towards which the Mohammedans look when
they pray.

Now as the hermit was an upright and pious man, and fervent in prayer, God listened to his supplication, and, vouchsafing a soul to this figure, made it an animated being.

Then the image, like unto a star in beauty, and symmetrical as the cypress tree, began to move, and to speak with tones sweet as those of the bird of night.

When morning came, and the four companions awoke, as soon as they caught sight of the girl they became prisoners in the chains of her ringlets, and as moths around the sun of her beauty, and began immediately to dispute and quarrel as to whose she was.

The carpenter said, "I first made the figure, and therefore she is mine; and as for you, you have nothing whatever to do with her."

The goldsmith said, "I have laid out gold and silver enough upon her to purchase anything, and therefore I deserve her, for I have made the greatest sacrifice for her—and, in a word, I mean to have her."

The tailor said, "I also have laid out a great deal for her —no end of fine garments; and, having thus contributed greatly to make her look so beautiful when animated, it is I who deserve her."

Then the hermit said, "This maiden is clearly enough mine, for she is the proof of God having heard my prayer, and a specimen of the houris of Paradise which God has sent me, and I have evidently the only right to her."

At last they agreed to go and have their dispute decided by the law, when suddenly they saw a travelling dervish coming towards them, dressed in the coarse cloth of his order. They at once agreed to be contented with whatever he should say, and to leave the decision of the question to him.

So they called to him, and related all that had taken place; but as soon as the dervish looked at the maiden he also became enslaved by her beauty, and began sighing like a flute, and thought of nothing but how he could get her for himself. So he turned to the four companions and began to say, "O Mussulmans, what nonsense is this that you are talking! Have you no fear of God, that you dare to act in this monstrous manner—some of you saying that you have made this woman from wood, and some of you that you have done so by prayer, while she is my lawful wife according to law and reason? If I needed, I might say a great deal more; but suffice it to say, that some days ago, a quarrel arising between us, she took it into her head to leave the house, and I set out immediately in search of her, and this is the cause of you seeing me here. Now, *El hamed u'l lillah* (thanks be to God), I have found her, and the best thing you can do is, not to make the people laugh at you by talking such nonsense as you have been doing, but to go about your business, and leave me with my wife."

So saying, the dervish became even more violent than the others; and quarrelling and wrangling thus, they came to a village, when they immediately went to the house of the Soobashi (chief mayor), and related what had happened.

No sooner, however, did the Soo-bashi catch sight of the damsel, than he also fell in love with her, if anything, more violently than the others; and he began to say to the five claimants: "O impudent vagabonds—you villains who murdered my brother, and ran off with his wife—you have come with your own legs to be caught, have you?" So saying, he became also a claimant, and they having appealed to the law, they all went before the cadi, carrying the damsel with them.

When they had explained the case, the cadi turned to look at the damsel, and the words of the poet were verified :—

> And lo ! a maiden of heavenly face,
> From head to foot full of grace;
> Tall of stature, light was she,
> Like unto the cypress tree.
> In every age hath woman been
> Cause of madness and of spleen;
> So soon, O soon was Mr. Cadi seen
> Prostrate 'fore this winning quean.
> The torrent of love where dashes he?
> He sweeps o'er the walls of philosophy;
> The bulwark of sense must down needs be,
> For in are rushing the waves of love's sea.*

The cadi immediately began to set about thinking how he could get her for himself, and addressed them, saying, " This dispute of yours is quite nonsense. I know this girl very well, for she was brought up in my own house like one of my own children, and is a slave of mine. As for these jewels which she has about her, she ran off with them some time ago, at the instigation of some good-for-nothings ; but now, *Ḥamd' u' lillah*, she has returned, thanks to your trouble, and I have found her. *In shallah* (if God will), the good you have done will be remembered by God, and no doubt He will reward you."

The hermit, however, replied, " My lord, is it right for you, who boast that you sit on the carpet of the Prophet, not to decide according to the law, and making up some tale about

---

* This sudden introduction of verses into prose is quite common in Eastern composition

this woman belonging to you, to take her from us? What sort of conduct is this, and on the day of judgment what account will you give of this proceeding?"

The cadi answered, "Think not to deceive me, O impudent old impostor, as you do the people, by your lean appearance and stooping gait. I know very well that when one has to deal with such an impudent rogue as you, one has generally need of all his penetration; but if you must needs lie, why not say something probable, and not such a palpable falsehood as that you have made this woman from wood. Come, cease this nonsense, and go about your business, or it will be the worse for you."

Thus the cadi abused the hermit, and the hermit the cadi, for a long time; and there arose a great uproar, until at last the seven disputants were about to come to blows, when the wise men of the city, having assembled in a certain place, attempted to reconcile them, saying, "This dispute of yours cannot be decided: no one can solve this enigma except by the divine favour. Now the Prophet (may peace be on him!) in his Holy Book has said, 'When you are embarrassed in your affairs, have recourse to the people of the tombs.' Let us go then to the cemetery, and you pray, and we will all say 'Amen,' and may be Allah will reveal this mystery."

So saying, they all arose, and proceeded to the cemetery; and as soon as they reached it, the hermit lifted up his hand and prayed, saying, "O Almighty and Omniscient God, Thou knowest which way this affair is: we beseech Thee to solve this enigma, and to let right be done to him who has the best claim." Thus the hermit prayed from his heart and soul, and the people cried "Amen."

But in the meantime, while the hermit was praying, the

maiden had leaned against a tree; and now, when the hermit had ceased, the tree opened in two parts and took the maiden in, so that she returned to what she sprang from, as the Arabic proverb says, "Everything returns to its origin."

Thus was the dispute decided, and every one knew that the four companions had told the truth, and their innocence became as clear as the day; but the deception of the other three was made known, and their faces became black. The four poor lovers, however, remained ever after broken-hearted and dejected.

THE INVINCIBLENESS OF LOVE.

THE old chroniclers relate that many years ago there reigned a great monarch in China, called Fagfoor, who had a vizier famed for his great learning and wisdom, and who was so much in the confidence of the king that he was allowed to enter the royal council chamber, at all times and at all seasons, without asking permission.

One day, according to his custom, he entered the royal chamber, and found the king sleeping on his throne; but, having made some slight noise in coming in, he awoke the king, who immediately got up, and, taking his scimitar, rushed towards him, and it was only with difficulty that the members of the council succeeded in saving him from death. When the king's wrath had somewhat subsided, they asked what had been the cause of the royal displeasure; and the king answered, that he had had a vision, in which he had seen a lady so beautiful that he had never seen her equal— nay, whose equal was not to be found in the universe; and that he was just enjoying the pleasure of contemplating so much loveliness when the vizier woke him.

" Now," said he, " the image of her is indelibly impressed on my heart, and the thought of her is inseparable from my mind."

When the vizier, who, as we have said, was a man of great wisdom and learning, and who was able to solve a thousand-fold difficulty by one of his happy expedients, heard these words, he thought of what means he could take to remedy the malady by which the king was suffering.

Now it happened that he was a master in the art of painting, and a pupil of the great Pahzad, and so skilful that it was almost impossible to tell his portraits from life. So he made the king repeat his description of the lady, and the place he had seen her in, and made a full-size picture of the whole, and placed it in a building, which he built for the purpose, at the meeting of four cross roads, just without the city, and inquired of all travellers who passed that way whether they had ever seen anything similar in their travels.

One day there passed a traveller, who, as soon as he saw the building and the picture, and had looked at it with attention, remained stupified with astonishment. The vizier asked him the cause of his amazement, and he replied, " I am astonished because this beautiful portrait resembles the daughter of the King of Greece so greatly."

At these words the vizier was greatly rejoiced, and immediately began to put more questions about the princess.

The traveller said, " Now, this can only be the portrait

of the princess, for she is peerless in beauty, but, notwithstanding all her charms, she constantly avoids the other sex,
because, they say, one day whilst walking she saw some
fowls in a thicket, and the wood happening to catch fire,
immediately the cock saw the fire, he walked off, and, leaving
the young ones, fled out of the wood, but the hen remained
with her young ones and perished in the flames.   When the
Princess of Greece saw the insincerity of the cock and the
sincerity of the hen, she believed that faithlessness was the
distinguishing and necessary attribute of the male sex, and
that all the insincerity in the world was among men ; so that
even the name of man was never heard in her presence, much
less the idea of marrying a man."

As soon as the vizier gained this information from the
traveller, he hastened into the king's presence, and related all
he had heard to him, and asked permission to go to Greece,
to have an opportunity of making reparation for his having
been the involuntary instrument of paining him.

The king gladly granted his request, and the vizier, having
changed his dress and made the necessary preparations for
the journey, departed, accompanied by the traveller as his
guide.   At last they came to the kingdom of Greece, and
entered the capital Constantinople.

The traveller obtained the vizier admittance into the royal
gardens, and the vizier, as soon as he had cast one glance
around him, saw that they were the fac-simile of the place
the king had seen in his dream, and knew that the Princess
of Greece must be the lady whom the king had seen there.

They, therefore, hired a studio in the town, and set up as
artists, writers, and decorators, and performed such wonders in
art that their fame spread throughout the country, until it

reached the ears of the Princess of Greece and the Emperor, her father, to whom it was reported that a renowned artist had come from China.

Now it happened that the princess was passionately fond of art, and asked her father to engage this famous artist to decorate the palace. Accordingly, the vizier was commissioned to ornament the royal apartments, and acquitted himself so well of his task, that all those who beheld what he had done were lost in wonder and astonishment at his skill.

At last, having completed all the other decorations of the palace, the vizier made a beautiful design on the wall of the princess's own private apartment. In the centre was a large garden, filled with roses, fruits, and flowers of all kinds, in which were seen nightingales, as if just in the act of singing. In the middle of the garden was a *kiosk*, or pavilion, of elegant form, in which the vizier represented the King of China sitting on a throne in all his majesty and glory. Near the *kiosk* was a piece of water, in which a buck was represented expiring in the attempt to save the young ones from drowning, while the doe was unconcernedly browsing by the side of the water.

Having finished this design, the vizier left the palace. When the princess saw it on the morrow, she was greatly astounded, and stood looking at it for a long time speechless, and at length gave orders to send for the pretended artist. As soon as the vizier entered her presence, she asked him what the garden, the throne, and the figure represented, and what the deer and the young ones meant.

The vizier at once profited by the opportunity, and said, " The garden is the representation of the private grounds of the King of China, and he of the noble countenance and

1

majestic appearance sitting on the throne in the *kiosk*, is King Fagfoor, the King of China. As for the rest of the picture, it represents a strange occurrence which took place in that spot, which has caused the king to detest and avoid the female sex ever since."

The princess asked the cause of this strange aversion; and the vizier said—

" One day as Shah Fagfoor was sitting, according to his custom, near his castle, in the spot represented in the picture, and was looking around, all at once he saw a couple of deer come with their young ones to drink in the stream. Whilst drinking, the young ones advanced too far into the stream, and were carried away by the current. The buck, unable to bear the sight of his young ones expiring before his eyes without his making any effort to save them, plunged into the water to try to rescue them, but in vain; fate having willed it otherwise, the buck perished with his young ones in the water. The doe, however, had not stirred, nor made a single effort to save any one but herself, abandoning the buck and the young ones to their fate.

" When Shah Fagfoor saw this, and the faithlessness of the doe, he said to himself, 'Ah, so it is always with women; such insincerity is only to be found in the female sex;" and from that time forth he has ceased to have any inclination or love for women, and abhors the whole sex."

When the princess heard this strange tale, she said, " I thought insincerity the characteristic of the male sex, but perhaps it is also of the female," and she remained lost in thought for a long time. At last she said, " This King Fagfoor whom you have represented, is a person befitting my rank, and it would seem that I was made to turn him from his strange aversion to my sex; and I wished for just such a sincere man as he must be. I dare say he would accept me as his wife."

So she went to the Emperor, her father, and besought him to give her to the King of China; and, although it caused the Emperor, her father, great pain to think of parting with his daughter, still, considering it for her good, he wrote a letter to the King of China, and despatched an envoy with it.

. The vizier and the traveller in the meantime returned to China, and reported the whole affair to King Fagfoor. When the envoy arrived from the Emperor of Greece, King Fagfoor, although dying with expectation, pretended to be unwilling, but consented at last to gratify the wish of the Emperor of Greece, as he said, to accept the princess as his bride.

He wrote an answer, and sent it to the Emperor of Greece, and did not forget to reward the vizier for his service; so that the vizier became more favoured than ever, and was loaded with presents and honours.

After some time the Emperor sent his daughter with her dowry to the King of China, and she arrived safely in that country; so that the king's wishes were crowned with success, and they neither had ever cause to repent their choice. To their dying day they blessed the happy chance which had brought them together, and left their tale as a legacy and an example to posterity.

THE PRINCE TAILOR.

IT is related that there lived once in the city of Cairo a monarch who had two sons. Having seen the mutability of all human affairs, and the fickleness of fortune, he apprenticed one of his sons to a tailor; for, said he, "Skill is always useful: and the wise men of Persia have very truly said, 'One grain of skill is worth a hundred thousand pieces of gold, for gold is soon spent, but skill never.'"

The prince soon became so expert a tailor that no one in the city of Cairo could wield the scissors and needle like him —in short, he attained such perfection in his art that his equal was not to be found.

After some time the king died, and the other son seized the throne, and would have killed his brother had he not fled, warned by some of his friends of his brother's intention.

As he went along he fell in with a caravan of pilgrims on their road to Mecca, and joined them. Arrived at Mecca, he was performing the circumambulations round the sacred Kaaba, when his foot struck against something, and, looking down, he saw it was a purse. He immediately picked it up, and, fastening it in his girdle, continued his circumambulation.

After a short time he saw an old man beating his breast, and lamenting, and crying out, "Whosoever brings me my purse, which I have lost, shall have the half of its contents as a reward."

The young man said to himself, "What could I do with all my father's wealth; of what good was it to me? What blessing has it brought that I should let this old man weep and keep his money from him?"

Thereupon he went up to the old man, and said to him, "I have thy purse."

"Where?" asked the old man.

"Here," answered the youth, pointing to his girdle. "Here it is, safe enough; fear not."

The merchant took the young man by the hand, and led him into his tent, when the young man immediately produced the purse, and laid it before the merchant. The merchant pressed him to his breast in his joy, and then opened the purse.

The youth then saw that the purse was full of precious stones. The merchant divided them into two portions, and then divided one of the portions again in two, and said to the young prince, "Shall I give thee the quarter with pleasure, or the half unwillingly?"

The youth answered, "Give me what portion thou wilt."

The merchant hesitated, and divided one of the quarters in half, and then said, "Which portion wilt thou have now?"

The prince again expressed his willingness to take the smallest portion, when the merchant said, "O young man, wilt thou take this portion, or shall I put up a prayer for thee under the golden gutter of the Kaaba?"

The youth reflected some moments, and said to himself, "Of what good to me was all my father's wealth and vast possessions? what now would this wealth avail me?" and, turning to the merchant, answered, "Go and put up a prayer for me, as thou sayest, and I will give up all right to the money."

The merchant immediately got up, and went forth, followed by the youth, to the golden gutter of the sacred Kaaba, where he stretched forth his hand and prayed, telling the young man to say " Amen."

At last, having finished, he said to the young man, " Go now ; I have put up a prayer for thee."

The young man left him, and continued his road. On his way he said to himself, " Wallah, if I return to Cairo my brother will surely kill me. I will go now and travel with this merchant to Bagdad."

Accordingly he went back to the merchant, and said, " O my master, I have come back, and will serve thee." The merchant accepted his offer, and so he went in the service of the merchant to Bagdad.

After he had been in that city some time, he said to the merchant, " Hast thou a friend amongst the tailors, for I understand the craft, and would gladly work if thou wouldst recommend me ?"

The merchant recommended him to a tailor, one of his friends, and the young prince went to his shop on the following day, and sat down to work.

The master cut off sufficient stuff for a kaftan, and gave it to him to make up.

Now if he had surpassed all the tailors of Cairo, how much more did he excel those of Bagdad.

He worked at the kaftan till after afternoon prayer, and when it was finished gave it to his master.

The master looked at the garment, and saw such work as he had never seen in his life before, and was prodigal in his

praises of the prince and his master. When the other
masters of Bagdad, too, saw the kaftan, they could not say
enough in its praise.

The prince's master said to him, "You have earned twelve
ducats," and laid them before him.

Thenceforth he earned twelve ducats regularly every day
by making a kaftan.

Now, one day it happened that the merchant quarrelled
with his wife, and in his passion the words "Thou art divorced
for the third time" slipped his tongue. When it was too
late, he began to think of what he had done, and bitterly
repented his rashness. He went before the cadi, but in vain,
the cadi telling him that, by the law, after the formula of
the third divorce had been uttered, the wife could not be
again taken back, except in case she were to marry again and
be divorced by her husband.

At a loss what to do, the merchant at last said to himself,
"Wallah (by God), I will make that youth marry her, and
then divorce her on the morrow, when I can take her again."

Thereupon he went and gave the young man the nuptial
gift-money, and, with the cadi's permission, married him to
his wife.

As soon as the woman saw the youth, her heart and soul
were poured out as water in admiration of his beauty and
princely bearing ; and the prince, for his part, no sooner saw
the woman unveiled, than he became enamoured of her as if
with a thousand souls.

After they had declared their love for each other, the
woman took the prince's hand and led him to another
chamber, in which he saw gold, silver, and precious stones,
and stuffs in heaps, and said to him, "All these are mine,

and if you do not divorce me to-morrow, and take me as your lawful wife, they will all be yours, and nobody can compel you to repudiate me.

" To-morrow, when the merchant comes, go and meet him, and kiss his hand ; and when he says to you, ' Come, let us go to the cadi,' say, ' What have we to do at the cadi's?' If he should then say, ' To divorce my wife,' you must say, ' Wallah, do we marry a woman one day to divorce her the next ?' If you speak thus, he can have nothing more to say."

The prince agreed to act as the woman wished, and the next morning, when the merchant came and knocked at the door, he went out and kissed his hand.

The merchant said, " Come, let us go to the cadi."   The young man answered, " What have we to do at the cadi's?"

The merchant replied, " Come, and divorce the woman."

Then the prince replied, " Wallah, what, marry a woman one day, and divorce her the next?"

Thus they continued for some time, the merchant in vain endeavouring to move the young man.

In despair, the merchant went to the cadi and complained ; but he was answered, " By the law she is and will be his lawful wife should he not repudiate her.   We cannot force him to divorce her."

The poor merchant pined and lamented in vain.   At last, consumed by the fire of grief within his breast, he fell ill.

As he lay on his death-bed, he sent for the youth, and asked him, " Do you know what prayer I put up for you under the golden gutter of the sacred Kaaba?"

The youth answered, " No."

The merchant said, " O my son, know that, however much I wished to offer another, no prayer would come to my lips but the following : ' O God, after my death, give the whole of my treasure and property of all kinds to this youth !' Now you see, O youth, that all I had belonged to my wife, and when I divorced her and she married you, it became yours. What little property of my own I have remaining, however, shall also be yours after my death; and may all persons who are now here witness what I say."

THE WIFE WITH TWO HUSBANDS.

IT is related that there was once in the city of Cairo a woman called Dalla-el-Mukhtala, whose history is famous in the East—in Persia, Arabia, Hindostan, and even in Greece. She had two husbands, each of whom thought that she was his wife alone, never imagining such a thing as that she had another husband. One of her husbands was a sharper, the other a thief.

Things went on in this way for some time, until, at last, one day the sharper came to his wife, and said, " O wife, my roguery has been discovered; give me some provisions, and I will leave the city for a short time, and travel."

Now it so happened that the only thing the woman had in the house was a cake and a lamb's tail, so she cut them in half, and gave him a portion of each; and the sharper, taking them with him, departed on his journey. On his road he came to a spring of clear fresh water, and sat down to rest himself.

A short time after the sharper departed the thief came to his wife, and said, "O wife, my theft has been discovered; give me some provisions, and I will leave the city and travel for a short time."

The woman arose, took the remaining halves of the cake and the lamb's tail, and gave them to him; and he left the city, and set out on his road.

By chance he happened to come to the very spring where the sharper had sat down to rest himself, and sat down also.

After some time the sharper said, "O young man, come and let us eat together."

The thief replied, "Very good, *Bism illah* (in the name of God)," and came and sat down near the sharper.

They brought forth their provisions, and spread them on the ground before them, when, to their surprise, they saw that they each had the same provisions, so like that they seemed to be halves of the same things. Amazed at this circumstance, they put the halves together, and saw that they exactly corresponded.

At last the sharper said, "No offence, young man; but may I ask where you come from?"

The thief replied, "I come from Egypt, from the city of Cairo."

"What quarter of the town do you live in?" said the sharper.

"Such and such a quarter," said the thief.

"And whose house is next to yours?" asked the sharper.

"Khoja So-and-so's," said the thief.

"What's the name of your wife, now?" said the sharper.

"My wife's name is Dalla-el-Mukhtala," replied the thief.

"But, my dear fellow," said the sharper, "the house you speak of is my house; and I have been lawfully married to the woman you call your wife I don't know how many years. What is the good of your telling such lies?"

"Oh, oh, fellow," said the thief; "it is like your impudence to tell me such a story, when, in truth, if you know anything about Dalla-el-Mukhtala, you must know that she was lawfully married to me many years ago."

Thus they quarrelled and wrangled a long time, till at last the sharper said, "The only way to decide this matter is to go to Dalla-el-Mukhtala herself; there is no good in standing here quarrelling."

The thief agreed, and they arose and returned to Cairo, and came to Dalla-el-Mukhtala and saluted her. As soon as Dalla-el-Mukhtala saw her two husbands, she knew what was the matter, but said not a word, and pointed to the cushions for them to sit down on.

The sharper began, and said, "Madam, to-day a dispute has arisen between us, which you alone can settle; have the kindness now to answer, and solve this difficulty."

Dalla-el-Mukhtala replied, "If I can solve the difficulty, say on; let me hear."

The sharper said, "In God's name, are you my wife or the wife of this man?"

Dalla-el-Mukhtala coolly answered, "Until now I have been the wife of both of you; but henceforth I will be the wife of him who shows the greatest skill in his profession, and brings me the most money. You have both been my pupils in the noble art of living upon mankind; go, and I will be the wife of him who shows himself the aptest scholar."

They both agreed to this arrangement, and the sharper said, "I will be the first to show my *savoir faire*, to-day, in the streets of Cairo; afterwards let the thief show his."

The sharper and the thief accordingly left the house. On the road the sharper saw a Frank count some gold pieces, and, putting them in a purse, which he put in his coat pocket, go towards the market. The sharper followed, and, cutting the pocket of the Frank open with a razor, took the purse, and, retreating into a by-place and counting the money, found there were a thousand pieces of gold. He took out nine pieces, and threw in his own silver ring, on which his name was engraved, and, hastening after the Frank, came up in time to replace the purse in his pocket. He then made a circuit, and, coming suddenly upon the Frank from another direction, laid hold of his collar, and cried out, "How dared you steal my purse and the gold . pieces, you rascal?"

"The purse and the gold pieces are mine," said the Frank.

"We shall soon see about that," said the sharper, who thereupon dragged him before the cadi, and accused him of having robbed him of the purse and the gold pieces.

The cadi asked the Frank, "How many gold pieces are there in the purse?"

"A thousand," answered the Frank.

"Thou liest, impudent knave," said the sharper; "there are only a thousand less nine; but there is my signet-ring in it, on which my name is engraved."

The cadi commanded the Frank to shake out the contents of the purse, and the first thing which rolled out was the signet-ring of the sharper; and, moreover, when the pieces were counted, there were only nine hundred and ninety-one.

At this the poor Frank stood dumb and confounded, and the cadi, mistaking the cause, reproached him with his infamy, and commanded the money to be restored to the sharper, and the Frank to be bastinadoed.

The sharper, exulting over his success, returned with the thief to Dalla-el-Mukhtala, who praised his address and the skill he had shown in the affair.

As soon as it was night, the thief said, "I was a witness to your stratagem; come, now, and be a witness to mine." So saying, the thief took a strong rope, and was followed by the sharper to the castle of the king.

When they arrived there, the thief threw the rope so as to catch in some of the iron-work at the top, and clambering up first himself, drew the sharper up after him.

They then went to the royal treasury, and having entered, the thief told the sharper to take as much gold as he could carry, and having loaded himself, they came to the place where the king was sleeping.

"What are you going to do?" cried the sharper.

The thief answered, "I am going to ask the king whether my skill or yours is the greater."

The sharper said, "Come, for God's sake let us go, and I will give up the woman."

The thief answered, "No; I shall not give up the affair until I have asked the king about it."

He then entered, and saw that the king was sleeping, while a page rubbed his foot, now sleeping, now awake.

The thief approached noiselessly, and hid himself under the throne. Observing that the page was chewing mastich, he contrived to insert the end of a piece of horse-hair into his mouth, and the page chewed up the horse-hair with the mastich. The thief then pulled the horse-hair, and drew the mastich out of the page's mouth. The page opened his eyes, sought for the mastich in every direction, but in vain, and then fell asleep again. The thief then held something to the page's nose, which immediately deprived him of sense; and, getting up, hung the page by his girdle up to the ceiling, like a lamp, took the king's foot on his knee, and began to rub it.

All this time the sharper had been standing at the door, and had seen all that had taken place from without, from time to time stretching out his neck, and crying, "Come away; for God's sake let's go. I will give up the woman, I tell you."

The thief, however, paid not the least attention, and, addressing the king, said, "O king, I will relate something to you, if you will vouchsafe to awake and listen to me."

The king awoke, and said, "Relate what you have to say, and we will listen."

The thief then related to the king the whole affair between him and the sharper from beginning to end—how they had entered the palace and gone to the treasury, how he had left his companion without, and entered himself, and how, after stealing the mastich out of the page's mouth, he had hung him to the ceiling by his haunches, and taken his majesty's foot himself. "Now," said he, "O king, is my skill or the sharper's greater, and to whom does the woman belong?"

The king replied, "The skill of the thief is greater than the sharper's, and therefore the woman belongs to him."

Having rubbed the king's foot for some short time after this, and the king having fallen asleep again, the thief arose and went home with the sharper, when he related to the woman what happened—how the sharper had given her up, but that he had, nevertheless, obtained the king's decision of the affair in his favour.

The woman praised his skill highly, and took him as her only husband thenceforth.

When morning came the king awoke, and the first thing that met his eyes was the page, hung up to the ceiling by his girdle. He knew at once that the person who had rubbed his foot during the night and done all these things must be the thief, and that the affair was not a creation of his imagination.

He was greatly astonished at the thief's skill and boldness, and much amused by his stratagem. He at once gave orders for the crier to proclaim, that whoever had done these things need not fear, that if he would come no harm should be done him, and that, moreover, he should be allowed to keep what he had stolen from the treasury as his legitimate property, and that the king promised to give him a regular pension of as much.

When the thief heard this, he lost no time in repairing to the king, and, making himself known, made a confession of all his misdeeds, and promised to abandon his former course of life.

The king pardoned his misdemeanors, robed him with a dress of honour, appointed him a pension out of the royal treasury, and he enjoyed the highest favour with the king till his death.

THE TALE OF A SKULL;

OR,

MOCK-MODESTY PUNISHED.

IN the country of Yemen there lived a merchant called Jerher-Shinass, who had an only daughter. As he was walking one day in the country, he saw a skull lying on the ground, and, picking it up, was struck by these words written on the forehead—

" This skull, while in life, was the cause of death to eighty persons.
This skull, after death, shall be the cause of death to eighty more."

When the merchant read this writing he was greatly astounded, and said to himself, "Well, this may have been the skull of some great warrior who, during his life, has killed eighty persons, or it may have been the skull of an executioner who has killed so many by his master's orders, or some great murderer; but how it can be the cause of death to anybody now I do not understand."

Saying these words, he took the skull and returned home, and, grinding it into a fine powder, put it in a hookah, and shut it up in a chest.

Some time after, having to go to a distant part on business, he made his preparations and departed. During his absence his daughter, whom we have mentioned before, came to the chest to see what was in it, and her eye caught the hookah, which she took out and opened.

"What is this?" cried she, surprised to see nothing but a little powder; and she put it to her tongue, and swallowed some.

After a short time she found herself *enceinte*, and eventually brought forth a son, which they called Ibn-el-Ghaib (the Son of the Invisible).

When the merchant returned he was surprised to see a fine boy in his house; and, on his asking who he was, his wife informed him of what had happened to their daughter. The merchant, remembering what was written on the skull, said, "It is in vain for man to attempt to avert what is written. Evidently Allah has sent this boy to accomplish what he has predestined."

Some years after this some vessels from the town of Sumak anchored in the port of the town in which the merchant lived, and some jewel merchants landed to dispose of their wares in the market. Amongst others, the merchant was a purchaser, and brought a number of precious stones home with him from the foreign merchants.

When Ibn-el-Ghaib saw them, he immediately picked out two, and said, "These are not precious stones, and are of no more worth than shells."

The merchant, believing his grandson, took the two stones, and went to the merchants who had sold them to him, and demanded that they should change them.

The merchants asked how he knew it, and he replied, "A young man in whom I have the greatest confidence says so; and, in a word, I won't take them."

Now, in fact, when the merchants sold them, they had not

K

known them to be false; and it was only after they had examined them with great attention that they found that they were so.

They at once fell at the merchant's feet and besought him to give them the youth.

The merchant, however, had no wish to part with him; but the youth begged him so hard to let him go that he at last yielded. "Let me go and see other lands," said he; "for, although it is true that you know my origin, the people insult and torment me for being without a father. Let me go, and save you and myself from their insult and abuse."

In short, the merchant gave him into the care of the jewel dealers, and, when the hour was propitious, they left the town, and started for Sumak, where they lived.

Now at that time there reigned over the city a mighty king, who had a wise and learned vizier called Kambin. This vizier had many slaves; but one, called Kamju, whose beauty was unrivalled, and who surpassed them all, he particularly favoured.

One day, whilst walking in the gardens of his palace, Kambin sat down by the side of a piece of water there, and Kamju, sitting down by his side, called her attendants to her, and they began fishing to amuse themselves.

When they had caught some few they put them in a dish, and presented them, still alive, to Kambin. Kamju, when she saw the fishes move, immediately averted her face; and on the vizier's asking her why she did so, she replied, "My lord, these fishes are still alive, and may be there are some males among them, and I would not that any male, even a male fish, should look upon me."

The vizier highly approved of her delicacy and modesty;

but the fishes, at what she said, leaped up, and fell out of the dish.

This greatly amazed the vizier, and he asked the explanation of it from all the *ulema*,* but none could answer him but one, who said, " No one can explain this to you but a youth called Ibn-el-Ghaib, now in this town, who understands the language of animals, birds, and fishes."

The vizier Kambin immediately sent for Ibn-el-Ghaib, and related what had taken place to him.

Ibn-el-Ghaib asked permission to be left alone with them for a short time, which was granted; and on the vizier returning, he said, " My lord, these fishes say they leaped out of the dish, unable to control themselves, at the hypocrisy of your favourite Kamju. Moreover, they say that you have forty slaves, each of whom has a private apartment of her own, to which she admits her lover unknown to you ; but Kamju, who was distressed lest a male fish should look upon her, exceeds them all in her faithlessness, and is the worst of them all."

The vizier went at once to the private apartment of each, and, true enough, he found each one's lover concealed there. He ordered the whole of them, the forty slaves and their paramours, making in all eighty persons, to be bound and brought out to execution.

Thus was Kamju the Modest punished for her hypocrisy, and the writing on the skull fulfilled.

So goes the tale.

---

* Wise men.

TURKISH PROVERBS.

THE heart of the fool is in his tongue; the tongue of the wise is in his heart.

2. Cotton and fire play not together.

3. He who is a man will extract bread from a stone.

4. Of ten men, nine are women.

5. If my station is little, I'm not oft in a pickle.

6. Give little, take much.

7. There are men, and there are mannikins.

8. The trade of the father is the inheritance of the son.

9. He who seeks, finds his master.

10. The man dies, and his name remains; the horse dies, and his course remains.

11. Old cotton is not made into wire.

12. An old shoe is thrown on the roof.

13. There is no news in the world which has not been heard (*i. e.*—There is nothing new in the world).

14. If you cut off the ears and nose of an ass, he is still an ass.

15. The dog who bites does not show his teeth.

16. The eye of the master makes the cow fat.

17. Weep for the dead man, and weep for the fool.

18. If promises were fulfilled, there would be no more beggars, for they would all be kings.

19. You may hope for a tear from the dead man's eye; but do not expect alms from an *imam* (priest).
20. Conscience is half religion.
21. Be a robber or a thief, but be conscientious.
22. Dinner first, and talk afterwards.
23. Think about a guide before you think about the road.
24. Death comes but once.
25. One may very easily pull the beard of the dead lion.
26. There is no remedy for what has happened.
27. If a great man should become a hedge, don't go over it.
28. Haste comes from the devil (*sheitan*); patience from the Merciful One (*rahman—i.e.*, God).
29. The great man has no friends.
30. If you mean not to work, fall in love.
31. He who cannot dance, says the room is too small.
32. Two rope-dancers cannot dance on the same rope.
33. Wine and women are two sweet poisons.
34. One "to-day" is worth two "to-morrows."
35. A thousand horsemen cannot strip a naked man.
36. A thousand friends are a little; one enemy is a great deal.
37. The tongue kills more persons than the sword; and although it is without bones, breaks bones.
38. Eat and drink with thy friend, but trade not with him.
39. Sacrifice your beard for your head.
40. With time and patience, the mulberry-leaf becomes satin.
41. Bagdad is not far for a lover.
42. A lover and a king accept no companions.
43. Every cry has its laugh.
44. Every one talks of his own troubles.
45. People do not throw stones at trees which have no fruit.
46. There are some lies which are better than truth.

47. Eat your fruit, and don't ask about the tree.

48. The world is a seven-headed serpent, which gives not one moment's rest to any one.

49. By mildness, a boy can lead a thousand camels.

50. A good horse requires no spur.

51. People should only ask about ages in the horse-market.

52. Knowledge is the best of all things.

53. The eyes are scales: the heart is a weight.

54. The elephant of India fears the mosquito.

55. The eye is a window which looks into the heart.

56. He who says, "I can deceive him," gets deceived himself.

57. An ant-hill in a plain thinks itself a mountain.

58. The dog barks, but the caravan passes.

59. He who spits at the wind, spits in his own face.

60. A sensible enemy is better than a foolish friend.

61. The honest man who speaks his mind is kicked out of the town.

62. We do not look at the teeth of a horse when it is a present.

63. If we have no riches, let us have honour.

64. More flies are caught by one drop of honey than by a barrel of vinegar.

65. He who gives to the poor gives to God.

66. He who wishes to live in peace, must be deaf, blind, and dumb.

67. Do good, and throw it into the sea: if the fishes do not recognize it, God will.

68. Patience is the key of joy.

69. Step by step we get up a ladder.

70. One learns more by conversation than by reading.

71. A green leaf is sufficient for a friend.

72. Tie up your ass first, and then recommend it to God's care.

73. The thief who takes care not to be caught, passes for a more honest man than a prince.

74. "To day is fast day," says the cat, who sees some meat but cannot reach it.

75. When you go to a blind man, shut your eyes.

76. There is a road from heart to heart.

77. Honey is one thing, and its price is another.

78. Who is the greatest liar? The man who repeats all that he hears.

A TURKISH LOVE-LETTER.

LITERALLY TRANSLATED FROM A MANUSCRIPT.

O H, EFENDIM!* may no woman launch the frail bark of her heart on the ocean of love! May no woman, far from her beloved, pine in the dungeon of grief! I am exhausted by long longing to see thee. Come! come! My soul pants for the water of thy beauty. O possessor of my heart! O my enchanting friend, my fairy-cheeked one, my sweet-tongued one, my nightingale, my branch of cypress,† comfort of my soul, joy of my heart, light of my eyes, wealth of my wealth, my dispeller of grief, thought of my imagina-

---

* My Lord.

† The cypress is the symbol of elegance and symmetry in the East.

tion! O thou of the cypress stature! O my coral-lipped one! blood of my veins, my own beloved,—the bearer of this, Raschid, brings you a diamond ring, set in gold, which I pray you may accept.

O letter, prostrate thyself in the dust in his presence, and give him the salaam. Go!

Unkind fate having made me distracted with love, I said, " If I write a letter, it will at least be a distraction, if even I should receive no answer ;" and then, having written it, that it might not be time lost, I sent it : and, hoping for an interview, and that you may think fit to return so much affection, I dared to write this petition.

In conclusion, " May the sun of your beauty from day to day increase."

ORIENTAL POETRY.

Inne min esh shiri hekmetu inne min el beyani le sihren.

" Verily, wisdom is from poetry, and there is witchery in eloquence.''

Lillahi kunuf taht il arschi mefatihula el sinet esh shuara.

" God has treasure-chambers 'neath his throne, and the keys are the tongues of poets.''

Words of MAHOMET.

ORIENTAL POETRY.

" Verily, wisdom is from poetry, and there is witchery in eloquence."
" There are treasure-chambers 'neath the throne of God, and the keys are the words of poets."

SUCH were the oft-repeated words of Mahomet concerning poetry, himself one of the greatest of Arabic poets. Some few lines, therefore, concerning the poetry of those lands which were the birth-place of fable and poetry, and in one of which the language of flowers had its origin, can scarcely fail to interest the English reader.

Oriental poetry can be divided into two classes—ancient and modern; the ancient including Chinese, Indian, and old Persian; and the modern, Hebrew, Arabic, new Persian, and Turkish poetry. The close relationship between the Arabic and Hebrew languages is nowhere more visible than in poetry, the Arabic poetry consisting almost entirely of songs of praise, lyrical, didactic, and descriptive poems, like those of the Hebrews to be found in the Old Testament. Epic poems and the drama were unknown to both these nations; and, indeed, the drama ever has been, and still is, entirely unknown in the East. The Persian language, on

the contrary, rich to excess in fable and romance, is no less
so in epic poetry; and poems of this character are to be
found at a very early date.   One of the finest and most celebrated love-poems perhaps ever written was originally a Persian production, afterwards translated, and even improved, by
a Turkish poet.

It is well known that the Persian romancers and poets had
such attractions for the people in his time, that Mahomet,
jealous of their power, thought it necessary to write a chapter
of the Koran expressly against them; hence the false idea
that Mahomet was opposed to poetry, which he could hardly
be, seeing he was one of the first of Arabic poets himself,
and that the most pious Mussulmans have always had the
greatest admiration and taste for poetry, and cultivated it as
much, if not more, than any other branch of literature.

The most common kinds of Oriental poetry are the *mesnevi*,
i. e., a double rhymed poem, which is generally historical,
ethical, mystic, or descriptive.   A perfect Oriental epic con-
sists of nine parts.   The first part is devoted to the praise of
God, and prayers to him; the second, to prayers for the
Prophet and his family; the third is a song on Mahomet's
ascension; the fourth, the praise of the reigning sultan; the
fifth, of his vizier; the sixth, a dissertation on the blessing
of the faculty of speech; the seventh, the reason for writing
the book; the eighth, the book itself; and the ninth, the
conclusion, the poet's excuses, the date, &c.   The *kassidet* is
a kind of long lyrical poem, and is generally used for pane-

gyrics and laments. The *ghazel* is a kind of short poem, consisting of not less than five, and not more than seven distiches, and is used for heroic, allegorical, and mystical subjects.

All Oriental poetry is characterized by hyperbolical metaphor. The Orientals, indeed, give themselves unbounded license in this respect, so that, if we look upon Oriental poetry with a critical European eye, it will often appear outrageous; but it must be admitted, on the other hand, that some of their poems, in richness, originality, and beauty of imagery, are unequalled.

The poetry of the Persians is, of all Oriental poetry, the richest and best, and comes nearest to that of the West, which is very natural, seeing Persian is a relation, although a very distant one, of European languages, while Arabic and Turkish have no common origin or connexion whatever with European tongues. The Turks, although they owe a great part of their poetry to the Arabic and Persian languages, have worshipped the Muses with no less zeal; and all classes of society—sultan, prince, vizier, and mufti—have been contributors to the divans, or collections of poems, in which branch of literature Turkish can number six hundred authors.

Murad II., the victor of Varna, made verses, and held assemblies regularly at his court, where men of letters, and poets in particular, were invited to attend, and encouraged to compete with each other in writing on scientific subjects and the composition of poetry, for which they were rewarded by

dresses of honour, presents of money, and pensions. His
son had regularly thirty poets in his pension, and distinguished himself no less by the encouragement he gave to men
of letters, than by the number of mosques and academies, for
having founded which he is so justly celebrated. He is said to
have given a regular annuity of one thousand ducats to Jami
and other Persian poets, continued to them by his son after his
death. The unfortunate Selim III. was the last of the sultan
poets, and wrote several "laments" while in prison. We
must not forget to mention, that the Turkish ladies, spite of
the disadvantages under which they labour, have greatly distinguished themselves in literature, and especially in poetry ;
and, moreover, it is to the Turkish ladies we owe the "Language of Flowers."

THE ROSE AND THE NIGHTINGALE.

A BRIEF IMITATION OF THE RENOWNED TURKISH POEM BY FASLI.

OF ages past, of times long by,
  Of an old and wondrous history,
Is the oft-repeated pleasant tale
Of the Loves of the Rose and the Nightingale.

In ages gone, in the youth of Time,
A Shah there lived in a pleasant clime;
And a good and a prosperous king was he,
And his people happy, and loyal, and free.

A monarch was he of prosperous star,
Whose fame had been spread to the ends of earth far;
Whose beauty of countenance, pomp, and array,
Have oft formed the burthen of many a poet's lay.

Of rule the most just, of character mild,
The friend of his people—man, woman, and child;
A monarch whose praises will poets e'er sing,
Whose rule was most wide, was His Majesty Spring.

*   *   *   *   *   *

By his gracious favour, and by Justice's rain,
Like unto the blessed Garden,* in his reign the world became
Far beyond the dim horizon, into lands far, far away,
Like the winds did reach his power, and his sov'reign rule
    and sway.

      *   *   *   *   *   *

And o'er hill, and dale, and valley, into every spot and place,
Ran his orders like as water, everywhere on earth's bright face;
And his goodness, grace, and favour, were in every action
    shown,
And by uprightness and justice was he to the whole world
    known.

In his kingdom happy, were there heard no sighs
But those of the *bulbul*,† as she sometimes cries;
And no fierce foreign foes ground the people down,
Though sometimes King North-wind took the Lily's crown.

True it is, that on his coming many a plant he slayed,
And both leaves and flowers helpless on the turf low layed;
Routed were the lancer Thorns, broke the Lily guard,
And the giant Cypresses trampled on and scarred.

And though virgin roses brought they, tribute on his path,
Could they ne'er his anger lessen, nor appease his wrath;
But this was the only foe King Spring had to fear,
And, though troubled by these visits, bright was his career.

Now King Spring a daughter had, and Rose was her name,
Whose surpassing beauty was the theme of fame;
Perfect was she in each member, and in look and grace,
And no words can paint one feature of her heart-enticing face.

---

   * Paradise.   † Bulbul is the Persian name for the nightingale.

Now it happened on one morning, in his happy reign,
That Spring looked upon his daughter, and himself could
    scarce contain,
To remark her wondrous beauty and her growing charms;
And he smiled upon her kindly, and then clasped her in his
    arms.

Now King Spring a province had, and a city famed,
Which the "Bed of Flowers" called they, or "Gulshen" they
    named;
And he took her to this city, and there made her queen,
Where in all her regal splendour was she daily to be seen.

And all Flora's ancient nobles at her court were found,
Where by love and duty to her were they each one to her
    bound;
And they vied them with each other to pay her their court,
Thinking e'en the smallest favour by such homage cheaply
    bought.

At her court, as wine purveyor, was the Morning Dew,
And the duty of the taster used the Nightingale to do;
So one night the Nightingale spoke thus to his brother,
For but this friend trusty no friend had he other.

" O my faithful friend the Dew, list to me and hear,
A great secret I've to tell you, which no longer I can bear.
I know that my changed condition marked by you has been,
And that your old friend's dejection by you has been seen.

O my friend, who could have thought it, and much less of me,
I'm enamoured of our mistress, of her gracious majesty—
She, the daughter of King Spring, and the Gulshen's queen;
I, one of her meanest subjects, heir to naught but spleen. .

L

She with whom the whole *noblesse*, all the world's in love;
She who to poor Philomel is so far above.
Yet most madly do I love her, for love-mad I've turned,
And love has consumed me, and my heart all burned."

Thus the love-sick Nightingale did his secret tell,
And then, singing plaintive ditties, from his seat down fell;
Still he kept on sighing and thus to complain,
Till he made the woods re-echo with his doleful strain.

"Love has made me mad," said he; "love's made me a fool,
And I've known no rest whatever since I'm 'neath his rule:
What I would from all keep hid does he oft make me betray,
And from the straight path of wisdom does he always make
          me stray."

"Speak not thus so dolefully," said at last the Dew;
"For, believe me, like you, lucky are the very few.
Fortune has for you yet many happy days in store,
Which, for these dark days of trouble, you'll enjoy but more

Cease but these sad notes of yours, and more cheerful sing,
And I'll lead you to your mistress, and you near her bring,
That you may regard her beauty, and thereby revive,
For I know her charming presence will keep you alive."

Now when love-sick Nightingale heard this from his friend,
He began his tune to alter, and his strain to mend.
"O dear friend," at last said he, "do I sleep or dream?
To conduct me to her presence do you really mean?

No more is my heart oppressed, no more do I grieve,
And for joy my very senses me begin to leave.
In this world and in the next may you be blessed thrice;
May you long live in this world—then in Paradise.

You have waked hope in my breast, and have made me live;
Take, then, all I have to offer—e'en my soul I'll give.
Take my body and my soul, and my heart and all,
If you will but near her bring me for one moment small."

Then spoke out the Dew, and said, "Act not thus in haste,
For in hurry and in scurry do we but time waste;
And you must have heard before that precipitation
Is the cause of all that's bad, and leads to damnation.

I will take you to the city, and near to the queen,
Where a friend of mine, the Cypress, long her sentinel has
    been;
There I hope to get you entrance, in this secret way—
And now, if you will me follow, I will lead the way."

Thus the Dew at once departed, and the Nightingale behind,
And together to the Gulshen did they their way wind;
And they came unto the palace, built upon a mound,
Where she dwelt in peace and quiet, all her subjects her
    around.

There they found the gallant Cypress on guard at the door,
And the Dew explained unto him what we've said before.
And the Nightingale, beseeching, 'gan his ills to trill,
And endeavoured to inform him how that love his heart did
    fill.

     *   *   *   *   *   *

He broke the stillness of the night with his complaints and
    song,
And e'en until the morning he kept unceasing on.

    *   *   *   *   *   *

When in the morn Queen Gul. arose, and from her sleep
    awoke,
Turned she unto her guard Narcissus, and thus unto him
    spoke :—

" Pray, what is this I've heard all night, and which e'en now
    I hear ?
Some one sings 'neath my window, quite to the palace near."
Now be it known the Cypress had to Narcisse disclosed
The secret of the Nightingale, and told him all his woes.

Then answered the Narcissus, " My liege, 'tis some poor wight
Who, burnt to *kebab** in love's fire, is in a sorry plight."
The queen Rose spoke quite angrily, " What does the wretch
    want here ?
And that he break my head like this I really cannot bear.

How dare he come so near the court, and here to prowl about?
I vow I will no mercy have on such a shameless lout.
What kind of bird is this ?" said she ; " and what tongue
    speak doth he ?
I'll teach the drunken vagabond the due respect for me.

Just tell him if he be not off, and this same moment go,
I'll give him cause to sing laments and thus to go on so.
How dare he come thus near to me, into the presence royal,
And, singing these low songs of his, the queen's night-rest to
    spoil.

---

* Roast meat.

Tell him if he dare to come thus so near to me,
He will surely rue it, and well punished be."
" My liege," said the Narcissus, " be not on him so hard ;
'Tis some demented silly wight, some roving love-sick bard.

And e'en, so please your majesty, he singeth not so bad,
And many ladies would have liked his plaintive tones so sad."
" Sirrah," replied the queen in wrath, " dost hear thou what
    I say ?
Then offer not thy arguments, but instantly obey."

Abashed, the poor Narcissus inclined his head most low,
And straightway to the Nightingale he turned to let him know.
Dejected and despairing, poor Philomel off flew,
And retired to the barren heath, where naught but wild herbs
    grew.

Here he poured forth his sad laments, and piteously did cry,
Till e'en he touched the stern cold heart of the East-wind
    passing by.
This happened on one morning in the blithe bright days of
    spring,
When East-wind found poor Philomel dejected down sitting.

Struck down by separation's blow, and worn out by long
    pining,
His former spirits were all gone, his state of health declining.
The East-wind close unto him came, and did him friendly hail,
And asked him very affably wherefore he looked so pale.

" Dear friend," said he, " what wind is it that's brought you
    unto here ?
For really 'tis a sorry place, and marvellously drear.
Besides," said he, " you've got of late so very, very thin,
That really to some great ill-luck you must a prey have been.

Your eyes appear to overflow with briny bitter tears,
Which, as they o'er your cheek down flow, wake in your
    friend's heart fears.
For such sad symptoms to account I can no reason find ;
Yet still them not to notice one must indeed be blind.

And that which me more puzzles in your dejected state,
Is, that you've been a-visiting the Flower-land of late ;
And as you have succeeded in such a land to come,
Pray, what have you to grumble at, what ill has luck you
    done?"

Then answered the poor Nightingale : "Although I there
    have been,
I have not been allowed to sing, nor yet our Lady seen.
The dagger sharp of sorrow has pierced to the heart,
And I'm going all to ruin, alone, from her apart.

The apple of my eye, my love, to see is me forbidden ;
And to forget her day and night, all vainly have I striven.
My sighs and vows affect her not, they are by her not heeded,
And no friend has her tried to move, nor to her my cause
    pleaded.

For if she knew the love I bear, my love for her so tender,
May be she would not be so hard, and e'en her heart surrender.
Now could you, gracious sir," said he, "just say for me a word,
I doubt not that you would succeed, and my sad case be
    heard."

" Fear not, my friend," replied the Wind, " and be ye of good
    cheer,
For I will be your messenger, and to her your prayer bear ;
And I will represent to her how it has gone with you,
And everything that's possible, I will to serve you do."

So saying, he departed, and crying " In God's name,"
He left his friend poor Philomel, and to the Gulshen came ;
And there before her majesty, to earth he himself threw,
And in his sweetest accents, he unto her thus blew :—

" O sun and moon of beauty! O heaven of delight!
May God increase your beauty, and make you yet more bright !
For a poor sick foreigner would I mercy crave,
Who, caught by your beauty, has become your slave.

Poisoned by the draught of love, has been his whole world,
And into love's precipice has he down been hurled.
Weeping the whole day and night, through the land he
        wanders,
And the riches of his heart on a dream he squanders.

All he asks, O madam, is, that he may be
Suffered in your presence, and your beauty see ;
This, in Mercy's name, you'll do, I do hope and trust,
Seeing the high cedar shadows e'en the dust.

And the sun and moon alike, give their beauty's light
To the rich man and the poor man, equitably bright ;
And I think you certainly could this to him grant,
Seeing that sage Solomon spoke e'en with the ant."

" Mighty sir," replied the Rose, " that's all very well,
But I must now pray of you to this beggar tell,
That if what he says be true, he must wait my grace,
And I cannot yet permit him to look on my face.

By long separation is true love but proved,
And by the possession is oft love removed ;
And the faithful lover has no will but hers,
Who is his beloved one, and whose frown he fears.

And should she e'en wish that they separate,
If he truly love her, he will his time wait ;
And if she should wish that he be not near,
He will never disobey, but this cheerful bear."

East-wind seeing that he vainly sought to touch her heart,
Gave her a low salaam, and turned to depart ;
And came to the Nightingale, and the news him brought,
That he had all fruitlessly pleaded and besought.

Then again the Nightingale 'gan to sigh and moan,
And out of his senses here and there to roam ;
And he 'tempted to be patient, conform to behest,
But he could find nowhere solace, peace, or rest.

At last, as it was written, it came into his mind
To write her a love-letter, about his state of mind.
Said he : " There 'll be no want of ink, for I my tears will use,
And 'stead of reed or feather, a long eyelash I'll choose."

He 'gan with praises unto God, as was there right and fit,
And then for the holy Prophet no prayer did he forget.
" My heart's love," then began he, " to lovers pitiless,
No cure for my passion, no solace can I guess.

Use your charms as you may please, but be not of them
    greedy ;
Grumble not to give the sight to the poor and needy.
Killed am I by separation, slain by sorrow's sword,
If I cannot waken in your heart some chord.

Have, then, on me pity, for for thee I pine,
And if I should perish, all the fault is thine.
Have I not, and do I not, e'er thy charms proclaim ?
Then really thus to treat me, I think it is a shame.

Have you then no pity ? would you thus destroy
Such a pure soul as mine—love without alloy ?
For I am thy poet laureate, and thy beauty's mirror ;
Turn, then, not thy face away—fill me not with terror."

Thus he essayed stoutly his ills to explain,
And her cruel heart to touch, and his cause to gain ;
And when he had finished, said he, " Well, now where
Can I find a courier trusty this to her to bear ?"

Then was there in Gulistan, Jessamine by name,
A young active postman, who there went and came ;
So the Nightingale forlorn did him this prayer make,
That he might this billet carry, and it to her take.

Now when Rose received this missive, and this *billet doux*,
Was she quite embarrassed what she ought to do ;
For, to tell the simple truth, her cold heart was moved,
And of love so faithful did she much approve.

So she wrote an answer, and his heart did cheer,
Telling him he was forgiven, and he might draw near.
With these joyful tidings did the Jessamine haste,
And upon his journey not a moment waste.

And when Philomel this learnt did his heart rejoice,
And he filled the woods around him with his merry voice;
At this change of fortune, and without restrain,
Did he make the woods re-echo with his merry strain.

Now there lived not far from there an old hermit surly,
Who was wont to meditate ever, late and early;
Hyacinth by name was he, an old grey-haired sage,
Who, at hearing these glad songs, nearly burst with rage.

Indignant at this outrage, he straightway then repaired
To the poor delighted Nightingale, and asked him how he
        dared
To thus disturb his nightly sleep and quiet meditation,
And what the cause of all this was, this nightly rest privation.

The Nightingale, all innocent, did then to him disclose
That he was only singing the end of all his woes;
"And when these gladsome tidings came, how could I then
        abstain?
Needs was that I should sing them—who could me for it
        blame?"

The Hyacinth replied not, but the next day at morn,
Went he unto the Rose's guardian, the harem-keeper Thorn;
Said he, "Sir Harem-keeper, pray what are you about,
To give such opportunities to every lazy lout?"

The Thorn, all in confusion, had not a word to say,
But steps, to stop such scandal, he took without delay.
He doubled all his vigilance, and kept good watch and ward,
And then before his mistress her folly he deplored.

And then to Spring his master he did the fact report,
Who, to hear such news about her, was very near distraught.
He gave immediate orders they should this fellow take :
"I'll make him rue his impudence, the shameless, worthless
  rake."

Meanwhile the Nightingale again had turned him to lament,
For Thorn, the harem-keeper, had him a warning sent.
Again he filled the air and woods with his sad doleful song,
Until he heard a faint deep sigh, of grief the choked sigh long.

"Who's there, my brother in distress," at last out loud cried
  he.
"Good sir," replied the same weak voice, "didst speak thou
  unto me ?
The Nightingale replied, "Yes, yes; come, tell me all thy
  trouble—
I'll warrant 'tis, compared to mine, a thing of naught, a bubble."

"Alas !" replied the Violet (for be it known 'twas he);
"If love be hard for thee to bear, what must it be for me ?
I, like thee, am left to pine—killed by separation,—
But have not the power to sing—that sweet consolation.

While with love for her I pine, and get thin and lean,
Does she not one moment guess what these symptoms mean ?
I cannot, like thee, to her my sad state make known ;
And my grief's the bitterer, as it's all my own."

While they thus were talking, came them then behind
King Spring's tipstaffs cruel, Philomel to bind ;
And then him remorselessly did they fast imprison,
Telling him from impudence had this all arisen.

It is true his dungeon was all gold and bright,
But all this grave mockery gave him no delight ;
There he lay repining, dull and sad at heart,
Thus from love and beauty ruthless torn apart.

But had been approaching, unknown unto Spring,
Near unto his kingdom, the great Summer King,
Who a warlike monarch was, no one could withstand,
For he came, with fire and sword, marching through the land.

And he sent a herald bold, whom they called Simoon,
Who went swift as lightning, and arrived most soon.
"Sire," said he to Spring, "I from Summer come,
And your only course now is, to cut and run.

Think not that you can resist him, for he is too strong,
And if you attempt it you will find you're wrong ;
Yield him, then, your kingdom, and make your retreat,
For if you should stop and meet him your fate is defeat."

" Who is this ?" replied King Spring; " who is Summer King?
Tell him that to boast him thus, is not quite the thing ;
As for all this violence, and this undue heat,
I will draw my sabre ' Water,' and him soon defeat.

He dare not come out to meet me in the open plain,
For he knows I'd cool his courage with my great guns—the rain.
Tell him he had better give up this campaign,
For it will to nothing lead him, but defeat and shame."

With King Spring's reply, came the herald bold,
And unto his master, this defiance told.
And at this bold challenge, Summer grew quite warm :
" This," said he, " from such a fellow, is not to be borne."

So he sent for General Sun, and him orders gave,
Saying, " My brave fellow, as of yore behave ;
Thou wilt lead the van, and now on—advance !
Spare thou not this fellow—use thy doughty lance."

Meanwhile in the Gulistan, Spring had made all ready,
Saying unto all the plants, " Steady all, now steady."
Marshall'd were the Lily guard, with their swords all drawn,
And with bow and arrow ready stood the sturdy Thorn.

And the stripling Rose-buds bucklers wore and shield,
And the Dew and River swore they would not yield ;
But as soon as Sun appeared, with his doughty lance,
Dared they not to cast at him even one small glance.

Broken was the Lily guard, though firm stood the Thorn ;
And their shields down throwing, Rose-buds were down borne.
Not content with this destruction, Sun did in his ire
Turn to clear the Gulistan, and it burn with fire.

King Spring seeing things thus go, and his sorry plight,
Took his daughter with him, and turned him to flight ;
And they found a safe retreat on the distant hills,
And a home soon made them, and forgot their ills.

Meanwhile, in the Gulistan, Summer held the throne,
And he killed the noblest, and the rest made moan :
Where King Spring and Rose had flown, could he find no trace.
" Here again," said Summer, " they'll ne'er show their face."

From the distant north, all this time, had been
Fast on Summer coming, the great Autumn King.
A mighty man in science was he, a patron of the arts ;
And in art and learning, man of no mean parts.

Spite of the old prejudice,* known as he oft been,
Unlike the great Mani, to paint gold on green.
Of King Summer's 'pressive rule, when they him news brought,
Said he : " Well, of no king, surely, could I this have thought.

We must take the Gulistan, and him from it drive,
And this kingdom govern, that the land may thrive."
So he sent his general, whom they used to call
The " Brave Leaf-defeater," and he scaled the wall.

Coming in the dead of night was his stealthy plan,
And the troops of Summer trembled, and then broke and ran.
And a thousand head of leaves took he contribution ;
And thus on King Summer came Fate's just retribution.

---

* To always paint gold on blue, usual in the East.

Thus old " Leaf-defeater" Pasha did an opening make,
And his master after him did the whole land take ;
Then for some short period ruled this monarch bold,
And all through his prosperous reign was no lack of gold.

Dressed were all his servants in rich cloth of gold,
And like dust in plenty lay gold-leaf, we're told ;
But as age came on him, and he feebler grew,
He became capricious, and his favourites slew.

Oft would an old favourite, pale and trembling, fall ;
Ragged and half naked were they, one and all.
Now, to mend the matter, came there from the north
An old tyrant hoary, out of prey in quest.

Called was he " Grim Winter," and when he was told
Of the tyranny of Autumn, since he had grown old,
White he grew with indignation, and to General Snow
Orders gave he to make ready 'gainst this king to go.

And so Snow right quick advancing soon the Rose-land
    stormed,
And the troops of Autumn routed quick as they were formed ;
Autumn, with his men and horses, soon are glad to fly,
And all o'er the Rose-land dead and wounded lie.

Then King Winter took the city, and with help of Snow,
Ruled the land with iron justice, and kept out the foe ;
And, although the land was dreary 'neath his ruthless sway,
Pearls and silver showered he freely on his royal way.

*   *   *   *   *   *

Meanwhile good King Spring, 'fore his enemies flying,
Had found in the south a sunny land lying,
O'er which ruled a sultan, of sway the most wide,
Who to the unfortunate was friend and guide.

And when he saw Spring, and heard his sad story,
Of the fall of the Rose-land, and flight melancholy,
He lifted him up, and did him great honour,
Saying, "Let not thy heart sink; we will help thee, our
    brother."

    *   *   *   *   *   *

In his suite King Spring taking, this monarch New Year
Bade his warriors to follow him, and seize shield and spear;
And onward swift marching, they soon came in sight
Of the Land of the Roses, the land of delight.

And when the glad tidings of Spring's drawing near
Were spread in the Rose-land, and that the New Year
Was marching along with him, him to support,
All rose against Winter as quickly as thought.

Old East-wind came forward to greet good King Spring,
And flowers came out trooping, and danced in a ring;
And the trees raised their heads, and gave signs of life,
Which ne'er had they given since the battle and strife.

Aghast, old King Winter saw his reign was no more,
And fled to the west, o'er mountain and moor;
And Spring in the Gulistan once more on the throne,
King New Year departed, and left him alone.

King Spring scattered largesse and pearls far and near,
And clothed in green garments were all subjects there;
And the earth seemed to smile, and the flowers to rejoice,
And the people of Rose-land to sing with one voice.

A bright crown of rubies the Tulip put on,
And the Cypress stood porter, as before he had done;
And the Lilies drew swords, and mounted on guard,
And the Thorn pointed arrows, and kept watch and ward.

       *   *   *   *   *   *

Again on the throne the Rose took her seat,
And the East-wind did homage, and fell at her feet;
And the ice-loosened River came out for the sight,
And the cup-bearer Tulip offered sparkling dew bright.

       *   *   *   *   *   *

Then bethought her the Rose, in the midst of the revel,
Of the poor Nightingale—the poor love-stricken devil;
And asked of her courtiers where and how he had flown,
And left all in the Gulistan quite silent and lone.

And then they recounted how he had been taken,
And thrust into prison, and left there forsaken;
And they told how he'd sorrowed, and kept to love truly,
And said, " You will free him, and pardon him, surely."

       *   *   *   *   *   *

       *   *   *   *   *   *

So she sent East-wind to seek him, and to set him free;
"And when you have found him," said she, " bring him unto
    me."
And the East-wind found him sickly, dying fast with grief,
And to travel quite unfitted, now that he had leave.

M

So East-wind his state reported to his virgin queen,
And she said, "As he has suffered as I did not mean,
Will I unto him in prison, my royal pardon give,
And tell him to cease to sorrow, and for me to live."

And when she his prison entered, and his sad state saw,
"Never will I pain thee," said she—"never, never more."
And the Nightingale, demented by her beauty's sight,
Said, "Am I awake or dreaming—do I see aright?"

Then he sang, "O sun of beauty, and the world's delight!
Fate has pitied me, 'tis certain, that I have this sight."
And to him she spoke most kindly, and to hope him told,
And behind a present left him—jewels rare and gold.

*   *   *   *   *   *

Then one bright sunny morn the queen rose from bed,
And donned a green mantle and turban of red,
And said, "Be this day a great day of joy;
Let no soul know of sorrow, our mirth no alloy."

And the Tulip was ordered to bring the dew wine,
And the Hyacinths and Lilies to form in a line;
And, the ground freshly carpeted, the world dressed anew,
Queen Rose issued invites to all whom she knew.

*   *   *   *   *   *

Then that morn came the Nightingale, and looked from afar
On the feast and the feasters, and his life's guiding star,
And, still of love thinking, of love 'gan to sing,
Till the queen sent old East-wind him forward to bring.

Then East-wind said, "Philomel, be ye of good cheer,
The queen has relented, and bids you draw near;"
And, when once in her presence, he was placed by her side,
And she spoke of the grief 'twould have caused had he died.

And she treated him graciously, thrilling his soul,
Till he knew he had gained a heart, and a heart whole;
And she poured out the wine, and they drank to love holy,
And she favoured him highly, and favoured him solely.

And Philomel trilled to her lays of love many,
And, save to regard him, had she not eyes for any;
Till the wine, passing freely, and all being merry,
Our bard stole a kiss from lips ripe and ready.

* * * * * *

And, as night came on, grew the revel but higher,
And in Gulistan feasting seemed never to tire;
There were Cypresses dancing, and Lilies lines forming,
And Violets, on tomtoms, sweet music performing.

And the Rose and the Nightingale's love grew apace,
Till the revellers departed, and left them the place;
Then their souls, by love's power, were into one twined,
And their beings cemented as seldom you find.

Then they lived a short season, a season of glee,
As loving and happy as mortals can be;
Till the Rose was assaulted and slain by the Wind,
And the Nightingale dust became, like all his kind.

NUVAZ AND BAZENDA;

OR,

THE PANGS OF PARTING.

THEN spoke the vizier, and thus did say :—
   In the good old times, a-lack-a-day,
Two doves there lived in the same nest,
Who from each other hid no secret of their breast.

Thus, then, they lived, and not one stranger saw,
To dim the heaven of their souls, or bore,
Like as the dust, which on a glass is seen,
To dim the mirror of their souls with spleen.

The waters of their being by Fortune left at rest,
Of the rich they had no envy, contented they were blest :
Like two devoted dervishes, in their quiet lonely cell,
In the corner of seclusion retired they did dwell.

Morn and eve they livened by soul-delighting song,
And to divers airs enchanting they warbled all day long.
The world for friendship we've resigned, as the poets oft do say,
Was the motto and profession of Nuvaz and Bazenda.

But Fortune, who e'er knew her let two true friends alone,
On whom the sun of amity had but one moment shone?
So glanced she then maliciously on these two friends so true,
And in the heart of Bazenda the wish for travel blew.

And thus he said to Nuvaz on this ill-fated day,
"My eyes'-light, in this dungeon how long are we to stay?
In the corner of this hateful nest, as prisoners in a cell,
Yet longer, how much longer, are we still here to dwell?

My heart's with travel-longing burnt—I am as 'neath a spell,
To see the wonders of that world of which I've oft heard tell.
The wing of travel let us move, and God's command obey,
To wander on from land to land, and in no place to stay.

The benefits of motion oft by others told have been,
And who can have experience, who the great wide world's
    not seen?
The sword of victory from it's sheath, from it's mate had it
    ne'er parted,
How could it on the battle-field itself so well comported?

Or if the reed* of glorious fame had in its home lain buried,
And never from its watery bed and dark oblivion hurried,
The words of wisdom in their birth would once for ever perish,
And the hope to live in memory-land we could no longer
    cherish.

The heavens which incessantly for ages round have gone,
Are placed above all other things on which the sun has shone;
The sluggard earth, however, which not one inch can turn,†
The meanest insect puny, can with its vile foot spurn.

---

* Pens in the East are made of reeds.
† Such is still the idea in the East.

The giant oaks so sturdy, which raise their heads so high,
Devoid of blessed motion, must 'fore the axe low lie ;
Deny not motion's blessing then, deny not what I sing,
For, by Almighty Allah, 'tis the cause of everything."

Nuvaz looked on him tenderly, Nuvaz gave one long sigh,
And the dew of friendship's mirror, love's pearls, were in her
    eye.
In tones of melting tenderness, in words of pleasant measure,
The precious stones of eloquence poured forth from love's own
    treasure.

"Oh, my heart's friend true," said she ; "oh, my shield from
    sorrow,
Never have ye tasted yet separation's horror ;
Never have ye dwelled yet in the land of strangers :
Little do ye wist as yet what are half its dangers.

Hear the counsel of the wise, words by sages given ;
Words that to impress on you vainly have I striven :
He that from his home departs, and sets out on travel,
Count him to thee ever lost, and gone to the devil.

The whirlwind of adversity, the blast of separation,
Has never o'er your corn-field blown, nor spread there devas-
    tation.
Travel is a tree whose fruit must be separation ;
Exile is a thorn whose sting has no consolation.

Hear me, brother," then she cried ; "hear me, and remember
That I told thee on this day, for our friendship tender,
That the soil of stranger-land—oh, that land of dangers,—
Is with hearts of travellers paved, strewn with hearts of
    strangers."

Thus spoke Nuvaz tenderly, thus spoke she for hours,
And the echo of her dulcet strains resounded through the
      bowers;
Everywhere but in his heart did they response find,
But his heart was firmly bound, and his senses blind.

"What you say," said he, "is true 'bout the foreign lands,
And that troubles wait us there numerous as the sands;
But yet, when a little while you this have considered,
From these idle fears for me soon you'll be delivered.

He who on his travels goes must expect vexation,
And the wanderer from his home has much tribulation;
Yet the mighty world he sees, and its many wonders,
And from sorrow's load is free while he on them ponders.

By the force of mighty use trouble's sting is broken,
And to such things, on the road, the heart's gate 's not open;
Soon one's soul is filled with thoughts travel 'lone can waken,
And one's heart by lassitude is not to be taken.

Who that on this earth has lived, the first day till now,
Has elsewhere gathered roses but 'neath the thorn-tree's bough?
Say, then, whatsoever, say then what you will,
Change of life is charming—travel's not so ill."

Nuvaz gave ear attentive, Nuvaz heard all these things,
And 'gainst these potent reasons she thus in answer sings:
"That you thus me should mistake cannot I tell why;
That travel has some 'vantage would I not deny.

Could we with us, when we leave, all our old friends take,
And no bond of friendship sever, and no hearts true break,
Pleasant would it then be o'er the world to stray;
Fain would I then wander all the live-long day.

He who of the feast of love can no more partake,
He who in the sight of friends bread no more can break,
Finds he in the busy world, and its contemplation,
One small crumb of heart's relief or heart's consolation?

So the poets of Persia sing, and their sages tell—
That the pangs of parting are the pangs of hell;
And they do assure us that they do exceed
Hell's most cruel torments, very far indeed.

Now, *El Hamd'u' lillah*,* have you all you need—
Home, and friends, and comfort, house, and bread, and seed;
'Neath thy hem contented, then, daring's foot in draw:
On this idle fancy meditate no more.

Take the hand of fellowship, and, oh, hold it fast,
Lest the bolt of severance heaven at thee cast;
Mark these maxims wise, then, maxims that are true,
For if you neglect them surely it you'll rue."

" Marry," answered Bazenda, " speak not thus so sad;
As I've said before, travel's not so bad,
Though the ill of parting, sure, be a great disaster,
Yet new friends to find again is a sovereign plaster.

---

* Praise be to God.

There is a motto old, if I right remember,
Which is very *à propos* for such love too tender—
' Why should we by this land or that friend set store,
Seeing there are many lands, and new friends yet more ?'

The bitter draught of parting has one small drop so sweet,
That you it—in aught else—never can such meet ;
Of the wine of friendship's longing, in deep pining's glass,
There's a sediment whose flavour naught else can surpass.

Though the dish of parting be not over sweet,
Yet it is more piquant far than aught else we eat,
And it has a pungent sauce, made of blighted wishes,
Which would even make it seem far above all dishes."

"As you will, then," said Nuvaz, "since I find you heartless ;
What avails to you to speak, as you are so faithless ?
You will find, when 'tis too late, that friends are not many ;
God forbid that you should find that you have not any.

False friends, it's true, you may find in plenty,
But of friends indeed, sure the world's most empty.
Never by the ill of parting have you yet been smitten,
And as yet the snake of flight never has you bitten.

Hence you think in parting's dish there's a pungent savour,
But when you have tasted it, you'll abhor its flavour ;
For, although the cup of parting be bright and full of glitter,
Mark me, you will find its taste marvellously bitter.

You will find the loss of friends right hard to endure,
And that for the road's mishaps there's no certain cure;
You will find the path you choose menaced oft by peril,
And above all number are the ills of travel.

Hear me, then, and list ye not to the voice of folly,
Else you will repent it, and be melancholy:
Shut not, then, the ear of sense, do not from me sever;
Dwell with me contented, then, ever on, for ever!"

" I have waited that you might this oration finish,
And with well-turned couplets long your discourse embellish;
But now that you've added up one side of the ledger,
Let us to the other turn and it well consider.

'Gainst all that the sages say and the poets sing,
Could I very easily this old distich bring—
'He that at the fire of travel never yet's been toasted,
Is like meat that's underdone, raw, and not half roasted.'"

"This thy fell intention will to no good lead;   ·
He who marries folly has for her to bleed.
Know ye not the son of folly heir's to naught but shame,
And the scoffs and jeers of fools, and the wise man's blame?

One small word of counsel yet have I got to give,
Which may you remember so long as you live—
'He who will not listen to what true friends say,
To the malice of his direst foes must often fall a prey.'"

Thus spoke Nuvaz lovingly to her Bazenda,
And no answer had he—not a word to say;
But he drew her to his breast, and her head there lay,
And he tried to soothe her, and her tears to stay.

Then the drops of sorrow's rain fell as in a shower,
And the wind of parting sighs echoed through the bower;
And with longing looks of love, that no words can tell,
Said they to each other, "Fare ye well! farewell!"

LOVE'S POWER.*

AND lo! a maiden of heavenly face,
From head to foot full of grace;
Tall of stature, light was she,
Like unto the cypress tree.

In every age hath woman been
Cause of madness and of spleen.
So soon, Oh, soon was Hassan seen
Prostrate 'fore this winning quean.

The torrent of love, where rushes he?
He sweeps o'er the walls of philosophy;
The bulwark of sense must down needs be,
For in are rushing the waves of love's sea.

---

* The above lines were inserted in the "Athenæum," of July 27, 1861, which says, "Mr. Charles Wells, whose interesting notes on an Arab newspaper appeared in last week's 'Athenæum,' sends us a specimen of Turkish poetry, which occurs in a Turkish romance. The translation is almost literal."

THE LOVER TO HIS HEART.

I SAID, "My heart, what art thou at?"
   "I am in love; but what is that?"
I said, "Come, tell me what it is."
He said, "I spoke not, if you please."

I said, "Just tell me, canst thou sleep?"
He said, "I never have that treat."
I said, "Canst thou her image leave?"
He said, "I can't its name e'en breathe."

I said, "When will this pain amend?"
He said, "When life comes to an end."
I said, "How are you, my sick friend?"
He said, "Fate's will we cannot bend."

I said, "What knowest thou 'bout fate?"
He said, "So much as you, Sir Emptypate."
I said, "My friend, don't be a fool."
Said he, "From you, that's monstrous cool."

I said, "My heart, thou art an ass."
Said he, "That's but too true, alas!"
I said, "Thou hast thy senses lost."
Said he, "I know that to my cost."

THE LOVER'S FAREWELL.

TELL me not that thou must leave me;
   Tell me not that we must part;
For the camel of departure
   Tramples on my very heart.

For if fate thus cruel crush me,
   And fulfil my direst fears,
Surely will the roads of travel
   Flooded o'er be by my tears.

When thou thus from me shalt sever,
   And to travel your way wend,
With thee will my soul go ever,
   And in two my heart thou'lt rend.

With thee on the road to wander,
   Cannot this vile form of clay;
But for thee I will this prayer make,
   And sincerely will I pray :—

O thou zephyr of the morning,
   Spread thy freshness where she'll go;
Murmur softly round her palanquin,
   Gently, gently on her blow.

Mayst thou never, never, never
　　Feel the weary road's fatigues,
As thou by road, sea, and river
　　Traverse dull and dreary leagues.

At the early dawn of morning,
　　May the lark thee greeting hail;
And when thou wouldst fain repose thee,
　　Lull thee may the nightingale.

Go, then, if thou must, and leave me;
　　But though thee I should not see,
Think not that for one small moment,
　　Are not all my thoughts with thee.

TURKISH LOVE-SONG.

OH, the dark night of thy ringlets has my heart made sad,
　　And the magic of thy glances has me driven mad.
Into love's vast desert pathless have I now been drawn;
And into thy dimples' hollows heart and soul are gone.

By the longing of my heart, and its deep devotion,
No time has it e'en to beat, nor the blood for motion;
From the hand of patience dashed has been discretion's glass,
And my case is now as hopeless as that of the bits, alas!

Like the mirage of the desert is thy pouting lip,
Which refreshing water shows one, yet allows not one to sip.
In love's deep, deep ocean, like as bold pearl fishers dive,
Mind, and heart, and soul together madly for thy pearl all
　　　　strive.

THE BUTTERFLY AND THE CANDLE.

ONE evening to the candle,
    Thus spoke the butterfly :—
" You revel in enjoyment,
    While if I touch I die.
To my darling light
    You are ever near ;
While dread death or parting,
    Am I forced to bear."

" Very good, my friend in sorrow,"
    Answered the poor candle ;
" Do not jeer at me, I pray.—
    Tell me not I revel.
It is true, I do not perish
    Like you, very soon ;
But at last I surely perish,
    And myself for love consume.

A single spark will send you
    Off into a fright,
While I stand and perish,
    And ne'er dream of flight.
This much I can do, it's true—
    I can for love burn ;
And if you did not know this,—
    Well, then, now it learn."

SERVE THAT KING WHOSE EMPIRE KNOWETH NO DECAY.

SERVE that king whose empire knoweth no decay;
  In that garden rose be where naught fades away;
Plunge but in that sea where you're sure to rise;
Find that jewel precious which deep hidden lies.

Ask the lover faithful if aught lasting be;
"Nothing," says he, "in the world, but its vanity."
Strive, then, for that empire that's not of to-day,
Which is free from changes and Time's ruthless sway.

Hear, then, what I say—hear, then, what I sing—
"Be ye conscientious, just in every thing;
For that heart alone is lightsome, and right free from pain,
Which knows no impurity, and is free from stain.

THE MERRY SPRING.

HARK! 'tis the nightingale!
  Come, let us spring-time hail!
    For joy's own bower,
    'Neath the almond flower,
In the spring-time's to be found.
Oh! hear the spring's voice,
And laugh and rejoice;
    For the merry spring
    On Time's swift wing
Doth quickly, quickly pass.

Flowers cover hill and dale,
Arid heath and smiling vale;
    But a fleeting thing
    Is the merry spring,
And ne'er may you see her more.
So hear the spring's voice,
And laugh and rejoice;
    For the merry spring
    On Time's swift wing
Doth quickly, quickly pass.

N

The groves are all bright
With Ahmed's light.*
Oh! people of Mahomet, come,
For pleasure's season's now begun,
And hear the spring's voice,
And laugh and rejoice;
 For the merry spring
 On Time's swift wing
Doth quickly, quickly pass.

The dew-drop gleams
In the sun-light's beams,
 And sheds forth the light
 Of a scimitar bright,
Of famed Damascus steel. '
Then hear the spring's voice,
And laugh and rejoice;
 For the merry spring
 On Time's swift wing
Doth quickly, quickly pass.

The rose and the lily in the fresh crisp air,
Look as blooming and charming as damsels fair;
And the dew on their leaves, the dew-drops of morn,
With fairy-like diamonds these sisters adorn.
 Then hear the spring's voice,
 And laugh and rejoice;
 For the merry spring
 On Time's swift wing
Doth quickly, quickly pass.

---

* A flower, *Nuri Ahmed*, Ahmed's light.

The season of sickness and death is now o'er,
And the plants and the flowers recover once more ;
And pensive and sorrowful down on its breast,
Doth the rose-bud no longer its sickly head rest.
    Then hear the spring's voice,
    And laugh and rejoice ;
      For the merry spring
      On Time's swift wing
    Doth quickly, quickly pass.

The clouds in their passage do every morn
The rose-buds with fresh sparkling gems adorn ;
And the gentle zephyrs, as on they sweep,
The earth in the musk of Tartary steep.
    Then hear the spring's voice,
    And laugh and rejoice ;
      For the merry spring
      On Time's swift wing
    Doth quickly, quickly pass.

The scent of the roses as it upward flies,
Meets the dew of the morn as it comes from the skies;
And together they mingle, and downward fall,
Every drop of the dew rose-water all.
    Then hear the spring's voice,
    And laugh and rejoice;
      For the merry spring
      On Time's swift wing
    Doth quickly, quickly pass.

THE MUSSULMAN AND THE CHRISTIAN MAID.

TO a dim remembrance
    Am I still a slave,
And its chains, I'll bear them,
    Even to the grave.
For such visions heavenly
    Must we dearly pay,
By most cruel torments
    Whilst on earth we stay.

Yes, my soul's enchantress;
    For one smile of thine,
Would be but a vile price
    Such a soul as mine.
Since that I of Paradise
    Had that fleeting glimpse,
Never have I known repose—
    Never, never since.

In an ill-starred moment,
    On an evil day,
To a Christian temple
    Erring did I stray ;
There I saw a Christian maid
    'Fore the altar kneel,
And what rapturous ecstasies
    Did my soul then feel !

Close to her approaching,
Unto her I said,
"Lady, my soul's mistress,
For thee my heart's bled.
Alas! that one so beautiful,
So fair unto the eye,
Should renounce Almighty Allah,
Or His glorious Unity.

Unto three gods praying,
Have ye God refused,
Who, in all things single, is
Through all things diffused.
Allah three to call
Is Him to insult;
From such conduct erring
Ruin must result."

Then in words surpassing sweet
Thus to me she spoke,
And her dulcet accents
Chords in me awoke—
Chords that to awaken
Was a cruel ill,
For that they vibrate for her,
Ever, ever still.

"Do ye not, then, God renounce,
And our Blessed Lord?
Call us not, then, infidel;
Teach not by the sword.

Do ye not, then, God deny,
    And His sacred Unity?
Remember so, that God the Three,
    Is a sacred mystery."

But just at that moment
    Came a distant sound,
And it loosed the dire spell
    By which I was bound.
'Twas the crier's call to prayer
    Which came unto me—
" *There is no God but God,*
    And no God but He."

THE LOVER'S ADDRESS TO THE LOVE-LETTER.

O LETTER of love,
    Of fortunate star,
The eagle of fortune
    Most surely you are!

The rose of grace
    Is your precious sight,
And your inside
    Is full of treasures of light.

You are love's hawk
    In the chase of the heart,
And the confidant trusty
    Of those torn apart.

The pledges of love,
　'Neath thy guardian wing,
Which heart sends to heart,
　Do you faithfully bring.

News to my loved one then
　Now impart,
And tell her of me,
　And my wounded heart.

*　　*　　*　　*　　*

Tell her of her lover faithful,
　Who for her all else forsook,
On whom now the eye of fortune
　Does not deign to cast one look;

Who is restless while thus parted
　From her by a fate unkind;
Who is fortune's sport—a plaything,
　Like her locks before the wind.

O my letter, like her eyebrows
　Are you also doubled;
To the world's joys closely shut—
　Never by temptation troubled.

You whose words are love's true servants,
　And to weary souls repose,
Tell her of her lover faithful,
　Who for love no solace knows.

Tell her, though she queen of love be,
  And though many her may woo,
Still devoted slaves like me, yet
  Are there very, very few,

Who contented are to worship,
  And before her throne to kneel,
And, enchained, yet love the victor,
  And for thraldom grateful feel.

Go now, letter, and God speed you !
  On your journey now depart.
To my loved one go, and tell her
  What I would to her impart.

Go where I would fain you follow ;
  Go and my beloved's will learn ;
Come and tell it to your master ;
  Once more, then, to me return.

CLAYTON & Co., Printers, 17, Bouverie Street, London.